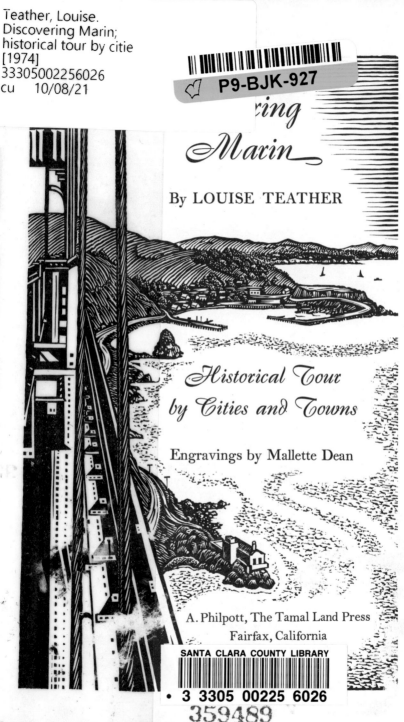

P9-BJK-927

ring

Marin

By LOUISE TEATHER

Historical Tour
by Cities and Towns

Engravings by Mallette Dean

A. Philpott, The Tamal Land Press
Fairfax, California

ॐ Mallette Dean's engravings are primarily of present sites; in a few instances they are drawn from historical sources since the original buildings no longer exist.

International Standard Book Number 0-912908-02-5
Library of Congress Catalog Card Number 74-77090

A. Philpott, The Tamal Land Press, Fairfax, Calif. 94930

Printed in the United States of America
Design and production by Arlen Philpott

For Dave, Jeff and Chris

Table of Contents

CONTENTS

Preface

Imagine the cries of approval of the Coast Miwok Indians centuries ago when they first saw the area now known as the County of Marin. Then imagine how amazed the Spanish explorers were, how content the Mexican rancheros, finally how aware the American settlers, in discovering Marin.

And discovery goes on to this day. Anyone who comes to Marin, for an hour, or a day, or to live, makes a personal and continuing discovery. The peninsula named Marin is the fourth smallest county in the state[1], but it is big in its varied and beautiful terrain – miles of shoreline, mountains, canyons of redwoods, valleys of oaks between grass-covered hills.

For modern discoverers of the county and its communities – as varied as the landscape itself – *Discovering Marin* offers points of reference: a little history of each city and town to show how it started, particularly in relation to what is still there from the past, and the origin of some of the historic names.

Parks, landmarks, museums and other interesting places are also here to see and explore, largely because within the last few decades there were those who took steps to save as much as possible of the county's natural and historical heritage. Today their successors work for open space, trails, bicycle paths and historic sites, to preserve the joy of discovering Marin.

[1]In land area, following San Francisco, Santa Cruz and San Mateo of California's 58 counties. Marin boundaries encompass 520.2 square miles of land plus 86.6 of water for a total of 606.8. Population in 1970 was 209,574.

Acknowledgments

A gathering of all those who cheerfully provided information for *Discovering Marin* and helped in other ways would fill quite a large room.

This imaginary gathering would include a number of persons who are intimately acquainted with the history of the county and local areas: Lucretia Hanson Little, Helen Van Cleave Park, Catharine Pixley Robson, Jack Mason, Dr. Scott Polland, Roy Farrington Jones, Peg Coady, Betty Gardner, Tom Barfield, Frank Galli, Rex Benson, Keith Collette, Romeo Cerini, Wilma Young, and Mrs. Thomas Kent.

On hand would be representatives of national and state agencies, county departments, the cities, official districts, the colleges and seminaries, libraries, museums, newspapers, organizations, the U. S. Army, the Coast Guard, and the Marin County Chamber of Commerce and Visitors' Bureau.

Present would be several who helped in special ways, such as reading the manuscript, offering suggestions and encouragement, locating places on the map, and answering questions: Joyce Wilson, Phyllis Ellman, Jay C. Crotty, Salem J. Rice, Mrs. Albert J. Evers, Nikki Lamott, the Rev. Paul Evans, Lillian Kettenbach, Virginia Borland, Charles Thornton, Philip Molten, and C. Malcolm Watkins.

To all of these, to Arlen Philpott of The Tamal Land Press, and to Mallette Dean – my heartfelt thanks.

A debt of gratitude to the late Florence Donnelly also is acknowledged. When Mrs. Donnelly died in 1969 at the age of 76, she left a legacy of many historical articles in the *Independent-Journal* for all who are interested in the past story of the county. Articles on two of Marin's most historic areas, San Rafael and Tomales, represent her work in the Bibliography.

LOUISE TEATHER

The Marin Side of The Golden Gate

Marin shares the world-famous Golden Gate and its graceful red-orange bridge – together with the fog which rolls in through the Gate and over the bridge–with the City and County of San Francisco. As Highway 101 (the Redwood Highway) reaches the Marin shore over the bridge, it crosses rugged cliffs more than 600 feet high. The bridge, old Army forts, and several historic points of land are part of the scene at this southernmost entrance to Marin County.

THE GOLDEN GATE BRIDGE: Despite the skeptics who said it was impossible to bridge the mile-wide Gate– first called golden in 1846 by the American explorer, Captain John C. Fremont – construction began in 1933 and was finished four years later. The bridge was opened to traffic May 28, 1937.

Chief Engineer Joseph B. Strauss made engineering history with his design for a bridge that is 8,981 feet in length, with the suspended portion 6,450 feet; towers that soar 746 feet above the water; cables 7,650 feet long. Men with buckets of paint named International Orange work continuously to cover the ten million square feet of steel; when they finish, they start all over again.

The east walkway of the bridge is open every day to pedestrians and to bicyclists who push their bikes. The west walkway is for use by bicyclists only, on week-ends and holidays only.

The name of the agency which operates the bridge was changed in 1969 to Golden Gate Bridge, Highway and Transportation District (adding 'transportation'), to enable it to engage in all forms of mass transit–including ferryboats, which, Marin residents are fond of saying, the bridge put out of business in the first place. In 1972 the district also took over the Marin bus commute system.

[13]

LIGHTS AND FOGHORNS: Warning lights at the Golden Gate shine from before sunset until after sunrise in clear weather and are operated continuously when the fog rolls in and at other times of low visibility. Under the latter conditions the foghorns start up to give San Francisco Bay its traditional symphony of yodels, hoots, growls and grunts.

The earliest light was in 1855 at Point Bonita, *Punta de Bonetes* or Hat Point because it resembled the *bonete* of the Spanish clergy. The present lighthouse at Bonita dates from 1877. It is not open to the public.

The first fog signal on the Pacific Coast was an Army cannon fired at half-hour intervals from Point Bonita, 1855-1857.

Bonita's light and cannon shots were too late to help the steamer *Tennessee*, broken up by the sea in 1853 off what was later named Tennessee Point. A shallow area off the point is called Potatopatch Shoal because, the story goes, old-time schooners lost deck loads of potatoes there.

The Gate's second light was installed in 1900 at Lime Point, named in 1826 by British Captain F. W. Beechey, apparently for its white appearance from bird droppings. Needle Rock nearby also was named by Beechey. Lime Point Lighthouse was automated in 1961 – a fate in store for other lighthouses including Point Bonita's.

The U. S. Coast Guard operates the modern lights, foghorns, buoys and bells, and the electronic aids to navigation including radiobeacons first used in 1921.

MARIN'S THREE FORTS: At the three U. S. Army forts on Marin's southern shoreline–Baker, Barry, and Cronkhite, named for veteran Army commanders–big guns guarded San Francisco Bay from the late 1860's until after World War II.

The importance of coast ground defenses faded with the growth of air power, and in 1948 the last of the batteries was dismantled. Some of the old artillery bunkers are still to be seen.

[14]

Supersonic guided missiles arrived in 1954. Today, of the approximately 60 Nike-Hercules missile installations across the U. S., one is located here.

Most of these historic military lands are now in the Golden Gate National Recreation Area. They include the three sections of Marin Headlands State Park, whose 660 acres were the first to be transferred from Army to public use.

Well known spots at the old forts are the Fort Cronkhite beach, rough but interesting; Horseshoe Cove in Fort Baker with its fishing off the rocks and dramatic views from just inside the Golden Gate; and Kirby Cove at Fort Baker.

The three forts are listed on the National Register of Historic Places.

GOLDEN GATE NATIONAL RECREATION AREA: A dream of conservationists for years—a great public greenbelt close to urban centers—was realized in 1972 when Congress approved legislation establishing the Golden Gate National Recreation Area. President Richard Nixon signed the bill on October 27, 1972.

GGNRA's scenic 34,000 acres stretch from Olema Valley south to the Golden Gate Bridge and then across the Gate to Fort Funston near the San Francisco-San Mateo County line. Most of the land, some 26,000 acres, is in Marin. Boundaries of the complex of federal, state, county and privately-owned land include:

Muir Woods National Monument; Marin Headlands, Angel Island, Mount Tamalpais, Muir Beach and Stinson Beach State Parks;

Forts Barry and Cronkhite and the western half of Fort Baker, plus the Horseshoe Cove basin on Fort Baker's eastern side;

Areas held for GGNRA by the Nature Conservancy, national conservation agency, including the 2,100-acre former Marincello, where a city of 20,000 people once was planned;

[15]

now renamed in memory of conservationist Martha Alexander Gerbode.

In 1973 the Marin Board of Education leased the Gerbode Preserve as an environmental education area for students of the county's schools.

VISTAS AND RAINBOWS: Vista Point, created by the State Division of Highways in 1963 on a high promontory at the north end of the Golden Gate Bridge, is a favorite stopping place for viewing and picture-taking. Access is only for cars traveling north; to get to Vista Point traveling toward San Francisco, you have to cross the bridge and come back.

It was also the Division of Highways that in 1970 decided to present Marin with resident rainbows–those painted on the south entrance and exit of Waldo Tunnel. ∞

Southern Marin

Sausalito

Incorporated 1893; area 2.1 square miles; 1970 population 6,158; post office established 1870 as Saucelito, changed to Sausalito 1887.

Sailors first discovered Sausalito. They were Spanish sailors aboard the little packetboat *San Carlos*, and the date of their arrival was to go down in history: August 5, 1775. First known ship to sail through the Golden Gate, the *San Carlos* found her first anchorage at the entrance to Richardson Bay, off Bridgeway at about Richardson Street. She departed the next afternoon and later sailed to Angel Island (page 30).

Whaling ships came next and for several years beginning about 1825 anchored between voyages in 'Whaler's Cove,' or Richardson Bay.

In 1838 the area became part of a 20,000-acre land grant named *Rancho Saucelito* (a derivative of the Spanish for little grove of willows), acquired by a former Londoner, William A. Richardson. The family hacienda on what is now Turney Street near Bonita was famed for its hospitality and feasts.

After Richardson died, some 1,200 acres of his rancho were purchased by the Saucelito Land and Ferry Company, which laid out lots in 1868 to begin the story of the present town.

Sausalito became the southern terminal of the North Pacific Coast Railroad in 1875, and ten years later had a population of 1,500 and eight hotels.

For a decade around the turn of the century, Sausalito was known as a 'poolroom town,' run by gamblers and crooked politicians, who were finally ousted by citizens' groups.

Sausalito continued as a major rail and ferry terminal until the big ferryboats and suburban trains stopped running in 1941. Not until 1970 was there again direct ferry service to San Francisco.

ALONG BRIDGEWAY: Bridgeway Boulevard extends from South Sausalito, still known as Old Town because the first settlement took place there, to Waldo Point on the north.

A local landmark is the Jack London House at the corner of Richardson Street and Bridgeway, where London lived and wrote around the turn of the century.

Along Bridgeway from Richardson Street north are stretches of open waterfront with a broad sidewalk and benches, accented by sculptor Al Sybrian's bronze seal on the beach.

Three vintage buildings are now restaurants. The Valhalla at 201 Bridgeway, built in the 1870's, was first a beer garden, then a saloon and speakeasy. The Ondine and Trident at 558 Bridgeway are in the former clubhouse of the San Francisco Yacht Club, built after the first clubhouse burned in 1897; the club was located in Sausalito from 1878 until it moved to Belvedere in 1927. At 588 Bridgeway, Scoma's occupies a 1904 building once a boat rental office and shop.

'THE HILL': Princess Street marks the end of Old Town and is one of the winding roads which take off from Bridgeway to what local residents call The Hill, where spacious older homes, some dating from the late 1860's, mingle with modern homes and apartments.

Distinctive buildings on these hilly streets include Christ

Episcopal Church at Santa Rosa and San Carlos Avenues, built in the early 1880's; First Presbyterian Church at 100 Bulkley Avenue, dating from 1907; Casa Madrona Hotel, 156 Bulkley, built about 1889; and the Sausalito Woman's Club, 120 Central Avenue, designed in 1913 by architect Julia Morgan (who later designed San Simeon for William Randolph Hearst) and built by Sausalito contractor A. W. Teather.

Another landmark on The Hill is located at Bulkley and Harrison Avenues: Daniel O'Connell's Seat. O'Connell was an Irish poet and favorite early Sausalito character. When he died in 1899, fellow members of San Francisco's Bohemian Club installed the bench in his memory.

BRIDGEWAY AGAIN: North of Princess Street is Sausalito's often-crowded downtown section with restaurants and shops by the dozen—40 of them in the four-level Village Fair, originally built in the early 1920's as a parking garage for motorists using the Sausalito ferryboats.

The building at 749 Bridgeway now The Tides bookshop dates from the 1890's and is said to have been first a gambling den. Later it was a newspaper office and then a plumber's shop.

Docked on El Portal between trips to San Francisco is the white-and-blue *Golden Gate*, operated by the Golden Gate Bridge, Highway and Transportation District. The 111-foot motor vessel began service in August 1970 as the first of the district's new ferryboat fleet. Connecting buses operate from a parking lot north of town (information: 982-8833).

Viña del Mar Plaza, a city park between Bridgeway, Anchor and El Portal Streets, dates from 1904 and was first known as Depot Park. The fountain and elephants came from the 1915 Panama Pacific Exposition. In 1960 the plaza was renamed for Sausalito's sister city in Chile.

The nearby Gabrielson Park on Anchor Street, dedicated

in 1968 by the Sausalito Rotary Club in memory of Rotarian and former City Councilman Carl W. Gabrielson, features metal sculpture by Sergio Castillo of Chile. Tiffany Park and Beach at the east end of North Street were named in memory of former City Clerk W. Z. Tiffany.

The San Francisco Bay and Delta Model, located in a huge warehouse at 2100 Bridgeway, opened in 1957. Built and operated by the U. S. Army Corps of Engineers, the two-acre hydraulic model simulates the actual bay and delta, complete with tidal action, for study by engineers and scientists. The model is open to visitors from 9 A.M. to 4 P.M. Monday through Friday and some Saturdays (information: 332-3870).

3030 Bridgeway, once the administration building for Marinship, is a reminder of the days during World War II when this 365-acre shipyard operated around the clock. The keel for the first Liberty ship, *William A. Richardson*, was laid in June 1942; by October 1945 the shipyard had produced 14 more Liberties, 16 fleet oilers and 62 tankers: a total of 93 vessels. At the peak of activity there were some 17,500 employees.

Across Bridgeway from Marinship was an industry started around 1888: the American Distillery Company. One of its products was Old Guckenheimer. A $2.5 million fire in 1963 which wiped out the distillery and thousands of gallons of liquor could be seen and smelled for miles. A proposed apartment complex on the site is named Whiskey Springs.

More than 350 floating homes make up the houseboat colonies at the north end of Sausalito just outside the city limits. Ranging from handsome to derelict, they are called picturesque, by visitors who like to photograph them, and a mess, by county officials for whom they are a headache. Along with the houseboats are several old ferryboats, some refurbished and occupied.

Four huge floating drydocks, veterans of World War II

service in the South Pacific, suddenly appeared in Richardson Bay north of Sausalito in 1966 and settled down on the muddy bottom. To a few people they would make a beautiful art center; to others, especially county officials, they are an eyesore and should be removed. Since they weigh about a million pounds they constitute a difficult problem.

Marin County Heliport, local headquarters for SFO Airlines, is located just south of the Richardson Bay Bridge. Big 26-passenger choppers make several flights daily to and from San Francisco International Airport and the Berkeley Heliport. ஒ

Marin City

Marin City was first developed during World War II to provide homes for employees of Marinship. At the peak of the war there were some 6,000 residents.

Redevelopment began in 1955 and in Marin City today are high-rise apartments, designed by architects John Carl Warnecke and Aaron Green, and given an award for design excellence by the U.S. Public Housing Authority; rental and co-op apartments; and single-family homes. Community leaders have taken an active part in plans for continued redevelopment.

Four churches are located in Marin City. The Manzanita Community Center was completed in 1968.

Some of the streets are named for county historical figures: Drake, Pacheco, Donahue, Buckelew. It was Benjamin R. Buckelew who in the early 1850's laid out the first Marin City at Point San Quentin. Unlike the modern Marin City, it was temporary.

Part of the present Marin City once was known as 'Gilead,' the estate of Colonel O. Livermore. In the 1880's the colonel built a large country home, kept horses, raised Jersey cattle, fruits, vegetables, and flowers. ஒ

Complex of Peninsulas

Strawberry, Tiburon and Belvedere, with adjacent Corinthian, make up a complex of hilly peninsulas between San Francisco and Richardson Bays. The combined shoreline of the four peninsulas measures nearly 17 miles. Within the boundaries of the two small cities of Tiburon and Belvedere, there is more water than land.

For nine years (1875–1884), North Pacific Coast Railroad trains ran over a 4,000-foot-long wooden trestle across Richardson Bay from Sausalito to Strawberry and along the peninsula's east side. Much of the right-of-way may still be seen.

GOLDEN GATE BAPTIST THEOLOGICAL SEMINARY: Founded in Oakland in 1944, the seminary moved to this 146-acre campus on Strawberry Peninsula in 1959. Pine trees on the once bare hills, flowers and wide lawns give the campus a park-like atmosphere. Buildings were designed by architect John Carl Warnecke.

An agency of the Southern Baptist Convention, the seminary grants degrees and certificates in theology, ministry, religious education and church music. Enrollment in 1973 was approximately 320, and the 76 graduates were from 24 states and five foreign countries.

RICHARDSON BAY WILDLIFE SANCTUARY: This sanctuary of nearly 900 acres in Richardson Bay between Strawberry, Tiburon and Belvedere Peninsulas was made possible by a huge conservation effort in 1957. Individuals, organizations, the state, county and City of Belvedere co-operated in a campaign to buy the tidelands and keep the bay waters open.

The sanctuary is operated by the National Audubon Society, which closes the water from mid-October to mid-March to protect migrating waterbirds. For the rest of the year the water is open to the public.

The headquarters site at 376 Greenwood Beach Road, used as a nature education center, was named the Rose Verrall Wildlife Sanctuary in memory of a pioneer resident who gave land for this purpose. Benches were dedicated to Mrs. Verrall and to Mrs. Norman B. Livermore, a leader in the campaign to obtain the sanctuary.

The photogenic yellow Victorian house at the sanctuary was built around 1876 by Civil War physician Dr. Benjamin Lyford and his wife, Hilarita. Daughter of John Reed, Mrs. Lyford had inherited parts of his *Rancho Corte de Madera del Presidio* including the Strawberry Peninsula. The house was located originally on the site of the present Harbor Point Beach Club on East Strawberry Drive, and was barged across the bay in 1957. Funds for restoration were donated by Mrs. Donald Ryder Dickey in memory of her husband, an ornithologist.

The grounds are open to visitors from 9 A.M. to 5 P.M. Wednesday through Sunday. The house is open during the same hours Saturday and Sunday only. (Information: 388-2524).

HARBOR COVE TIDELANDS NATURE PRESERVE: Located at the end of Harbor Cove Way on the east side of Strawberry Peninsula, the 11-acre tideland area was purchased in 1965 with a federal open space grant plus funds from individuals, the county, City of Tiburon, Strawberry Recreation District and Audubon Society. The preserve is kept as open space and as a refuge for birds and other wildlife.

'BLACKIE'S PASTURE': This has become the accepted place name for the field on Greenwood Beach Road off Tiburon Boulevard where Blackie the Swaybacked Horse grazed for some 25 years. Blackie died in 1966 at the age of about 40, was buried in his pasture, and a white picket fence was built around his grave. A marker was placed in one corner of the field by the Tiburon Chamber of Commerce.

Trains rumbled past Blackie's Pasture, 1884–1967, over a wooden trestle which spanned Tiburon Boulevard near the intersection of Trestle Glen Road. The trestle was torn down in 1968 but the remains of its south anchor may still be seen on a rise near the pasture.

RICHARDSON BAY PATH: The black-topped path for pedestrians and bicyclists runs for two-plus miles from Blackie's Pasture to the junction of Tiburon Boulevard and Cove Road, mostly on an old railroad right-of-way and mostly along the shore of Richardson Bay.

The path was built in 1971 by the City of Tiburon with Belvedere contributing, as well as the Northwestern Pacific Railroad and U.S. Department of Housing and Urban Development (HUD). In 1972, Tiburon city officials mapped plans for Richardson Bay Lineal Park, including the bicycle path, Richardson Bay Park, and Blackie's Pasture, the last acquired with the help of the Tiburon Foundation and Samuel M. Shapero. ⚭

Belvedere

Incorporated 1896; area 1.57 square miles (0.5 of land, 1.07 of water); 1970 population 2,599; post office established 1897, combined with Tiburon 1956.

The small, hilly "island" now known as Belvedere had several other names in the past. One was Spanish: *El Potrero de la Punta del Tiburon* (The Pasture of Point Tiburon), in the 1830's and 1840's. As the estate of one man, Israel Kashow, the name was Kashow's Island for 30 years, 1855–1885. A pear tree from Kashow's orchard still grows on San Rafael Avenue near the Belvedere Community Center and is marked by a plaque.

Kashow and his family were allowed to remain in 1867 when a military reservation was established under the name of Peninsula Island. Occupation troops were on hand for two months in 1871.

Eventually Thomas B. Valentine, a printer and land speculator, owned the entire island, and it acquired its permanent name: Belvedere, Italian for beautiful view. Valentine organized the original Belvedere Land Company. When the first subdivision map was filed in 1890, the island was launched on its career as a choice summer colony and then as one of the Bay Area's select suburban communities— and the smallest incorporated city in Marin.

Early Belvedere gained a reputation for wealth and fine homes; for fun and frolic at the Belvedere Hotel on Belvedere Cove, where Kashow's home had been and the San Francisco Yacht Club is today; for elegant and some not so elegant arks (houseboats) along the shores and in the cove and lagoon. The original large lagoon stretched from the present San Rafael Avenue to Mar West Street and Main Street in Tiburon. Filling began in the mid-1920's, and today's Belvedere Lagoon residential area with its modern homes fronting the water was developed starting in the 1940's.

One of Belvedere's 19th century arks that survived is now at the State Maritime Historical Park near Fisherman's Wharf in San Francisco. Donated by Admiral and Mrs. Robert P. Lewis, the ark was moved and restored with funds given by Mrs. Harry B. Allen.

Open water around Belvedere includes that of Richardson Bay west of San Rafael Avenue, where tidelands were purchased in 1954 with funds raised by local residents and deeded to the city. The Belvedere Land Company added more acreage. The tidelands are contiguous to those of the Richardson Bay Wildlife Sanctuary.

Belvedere Community Center on San Rafael Avenue is a former Presbyterian Church built in the late 1890's. Moved in 1949 from its original location at Bayview and Laurel Avenues, the building was remodeled to house city offices and council chambers, with a firehouse on the lower level. Land for the adjacent Belvedere Community Park, dedicated in 1958, was donated by the late Harry B. Allen. ๛

Tiburon

Incorporated 1964; area 13.8 square miles (3.6 of land including 1.0 on Angel Island, 10.2 of water); 1970 population 6,209; post office established 1884, combined with Belvedere 1956.

'Tiburon' is one of Marin's oldest place names, derived from the Spanish *Punta de Tiburon* or Shark Point. The incorporated city named Tiburon is Marin's newest.

Today's community evolved from a waterfront settlement on the southeast tip of the peninsula created in 1884 when Colonel Peter Donahue brought in a branch line of his San Francisco and North Pacific Railroad from San Rafael, and connected the trains with big ferryboats to and from San Francisco.

Two of the ferryboats were built in the local yards: the *Tiburon* (1884) and the *Ukiah* (1890). The former is long gone but the latter, rebuilt in 1923 and renamed *Eureka*, is preserved at the San Francisco State Maritime Historical Park.

The big ferryboats out of Tiburon lasted until 1909 and shuttle service on a smaller boat via Sausalito until 1934. An attempt to restore ferries direct to San Francisco was made in 1929 by the then-new Tiburon Chamber of Commerce. No ferryboats materialized, but an extension of Tiburon Boulevard did, from San Rafael Avenue to Main Street, straight down the peninsula on filled land once part of the old lagoon (page 25). The last half-mile of the extension is now the main road through downtown Tiburon.

In 1962 ferry service to and from San Francisco was finally restored on the Harbor Carriers' red-and-white fleet (information: 398-1141).

Tiburon's railroad days ended in 1967 when the last freight train pulled out, and the once-busy yards are now abandoned and awaiting development except for a few buildings converted to other uses. Still standing on the waterfront is the old depot, now the Peter Donahue Building at 1920 Paradise Drive, remodeled for offices.

Today the former railroad town of Tiburon is a suburban community spread over most of the long peninsula. The area on Mar West Street above the old railroad yards, where the first homes were built, is sometimes called Old Town. At 2036 Paradise Drive the stone Lyford's Tower remains as a landmark from the first subdivision, Lyford's Hygeia, laid out in the 1880's by Dr. Benjamin Lyford.

The name of Dr. Lyford's wife, Hilarita, was given to a railway station which stood near the site of the present housing development also named Hilarita.

MAIN STREET: In the early 1880's, Main Street sprouted on the fringe of the railroad yards to provide the general store, post office, hotels and saloons for the new town. This remained the area business hub for 70 years despite fires, storms, and the rowdy bootleg days of Prohibition.

The street survived the shift in the downtown business center away from the waterfront starting in the mid-1950's with opening of the Boardwalk, nucleus of the present commercial area along Tiburon Boulevard. Main Street today is a salty tourist center packed with restaurants, bars and shops. Probably the only building to have survived numerous fires is 13–15–17 Main Street, dating from the 1890's; a more recent addition fronts the sidewalk and a compass rose decorates the false front of the original structure.

Entrance to the Corinthian Yacht Club, located partly in Tiburon and partly in Belvedere, is from Main Street. The club dates from 1886.

OLD ST. HILARY'S HISTORIC PRESERVE: The focal point of this four-acre site on a hill above downtown Tiburon is a little white 'Carpenter's Gothic' former church, Old St.

Hilary's, built in 1888 as the first church in the area, and until 1954 used for Catholic services. In 1959 the Belvedere-Tiburon Landmarks Society purchased Old St. Hilary's and then, to preserve rare wildflowers, added more land with donations, a federal open space grant, and funds from the county and the cities of Tiburon and Belvedere.

Areas in the preserve are the John Thomas Howell Botanical Garden, named for the curator emeritus of botany at the California Academy of Sciences; Caroline S. Livermore Vista Point, for the late conservation leader; and Dakin Lane, named in memory of the Landmarks Society's first benefactor, Susanna Bryant Dakin, and her family.

The lane and old church site are owned by the society; title to the remainder is held by the county, which counts the preserve in the county parks system. The Landmarks Society is administrator.

A total of 210 plant species grow in the preserve. They include the Tiburon Paintbrush and Black Jewel Flower, found nowhere else in the world but on the Tiburon Peninsula.

The preserve was Marin's first state-registered Point of Historic Interest: Marin 00-1.

Old St. Hilary's is open to visitors as a museum on local history and botany from 1 to 4 P.M. Sundays and Wednesdays, April 1– October 1. Exhibits, concerts and weddings also take place in the old church.

ANGEL ISLAND STATE PARK (State Historical Landmark No. 529): Any pageant depicting the history of this 740-acre island would take an enormous cast of characters: Coast Miwok Indians, Spanish explorers, Russian sea otter hunters, Mexican-California *rancheros*, American soldiers, German prisoners-of-war, Oriental immigrants, and more.

The Indians met the Spanish packetboat *San Carlos* when she sailed into Ayala Cove on August 13, 1775, with an exploring party assigned to conduct the first survey of San Francisco Bay. The ship anchored in the cove for 25 days. Her commander, Lieut. Juan Manuel de Ayala, named the island *Isla de los Angeles*.

In 1814 the British sloop-of-war *Racoon* was a visitor and left her name with the straits between the island and Tiburon mainland.

Thousands of soldiers were stationed on the island from 1863 through World War II. Still to be seen are remains of old gun batteries; Civil War-vintage buildings, plus a big brick warehouse built in 1908, at Camp Reynolds (West Garrison); and the Mission-style Army complex at East Garrison dating from the early 1900's. There was a guided missile installation above Point Blunt, 1955–1962.

North Garrison (Winslow Cove) was used by the U.S. Immigration Service, 1905–1941, and Ayala Cove for a U.S. Public Health Service Quarantine Station, 1888–1949. Ayala Cove formerly was called Hospital Cove.

The state park was created starting in 1955 at the urging of conservationists, including Mrs. Norman B. (Caroline)

Livermore, for whom the highest peak (781 feet) was named, and Charles W. Winslow, for whom a cove was named.

Dedication of the island as a state historical landmark took place in 1970 during the second annual Tiburon civic celebration called Ayala Day. The National Park Service lists the island on its National Register of Historic Places.

Ayala Cove is the location of park headquarters, in the former Quarantine Station bachelor dormitory, with a Visitor Center in the same building. The island's only public docking and mooring facilities also are in this cove.

Twelve miles of trails start at Ayala Cove. From spring through early fall, bicycles may be rented in the cove and visitors may board an open-coach elephant train for a six-mile tour of the island. There are picnic areas in Ayala Cove, at Camp Reynolds and East Garrison.

This unique island state park, open daily until sunset the year around, is a favorite spot for a day's outing for Marin residents and visitors alike. Ferries operate from Tiburon (Angel Island State Park Ferry: 435-2131), San Francisco and Berkeley (Harbor Carriers: 398-1141).

NOAA MARINE RESEARCH CENTER: The Tiburon Fisheries Laboratory, operated by the National Oceanic and Atmospheric Administration (NOAA) of the U.S. Department of Commerce, is located two and a half miles—and 41 curves—east of downtown Tiburon at 3150 Paradise Drive.

Research by laboratory scientists concerns fishery resources in the Pacific coastal zone, their environment, and the effects of man's activities on these resources.

A second laboratory, the Marine Minerals Technology Center, was closed in March of 1973.

This area's long history goes back to 1877 as a codfish plant, U.S. Navy Coaling Station (1904), first location of the California Maritime Academy (1931), and Tiburon Naval Net Depot (1940–1958.) Marine research began in 1961 at what was first known as the Tiburon Oceanographic Center.

For years the area was called California City, using the name given by Benjamin R. Buckelew in 1852 to a 320-acre tract fronting the bay at what is now Paradise Cay, three miles north. The latter site was where Buckelew first dreamed of a new city. When it seemed doomed to failure he moved to San Quentin Point (page 63).

TIBURON UPLANDS NATURE PRESERVE: After the Tiburon Naval Net Depot closed in 1958, the county acquired part of the site for this preserve. Its 24 acres of steep hillside are located across Paradise Drive from the NOAA Center. Held as open space, the preserve is accessible only by hiking.

PARADISE BEACH COUNTY PARK: The Floating Dry Dock Training Center, added to the Tiburon Net Depot during World War II, is now an 18-acre park on San Francisco Bay. The land was acquired by the county in 1959. Features of the park are a long fishing pier, picnic areas, distinctive landscaping—and views. ∽

Mill Valley

Incorporated 1900; area 4.7 square miles; 1970 population 12,942; post office established 1890, known as Eastland 1892–1904.

Mill Valley acquired its name naturally: this was the valley in the redwoods at the base of Mount Tamalpais where a sawmill was built in 1836 by pioneer John Reed. The mill, minus its waterwheel, still stands in Old Mill City Park and is a state historical landmark. Reed's adobe home at what is now LaGoma Street and Locke Lane crumbled away, but four twisted almond trees from his orchard remain at LaGoma and Sycamore.

John Reed was the recipient in 1834 of Marin's first land grant, *Rancho Corte de Madera del Presidio* (Cut Wood for the Presidio), but his sawmill site on Cascade (Old Mill) Creek turned out later to be in the adjacent grant, *Rancho Saucelito*.

Mill Valley's first subdivision also was on the *Rancho Saucelito* side; it included most of the present central downtown area west of Miller and West Blithedale Avenues. When lots were auctioned by the Tamalpais Land and Water Company in 1890 at a big picnic near the old sawmill, buyers arrived on a new branch line of the North Pacific Coast Railroad.

The company's choice of a name for the new town was Eastland, for one of its officials, Joseph G. Eastland, but many residents preferred Mill Valley. For a dozen years both names appeared on the sign at the railroad station.

Samuel P. Throckmorton, administrator of *Rancho Saucelito* in its last years, left his name with a principal avenue and the name of his hunting lodge, The Homestead, with an adjacent valley. Miller Avenue was named for C. O. G. Miller, a banker who helped in the original town development.

Mill Valley's earliest resort hotel was the Blithedale, built in 1879 at what is now 205 West Blithedale Avenue. (Vacationers of the 1880's knew the whole area as 'Blithedale'.) In the 1890's other hotels appeared, plus tents, cottages and the first homes, some big and luxurious. Residents of the early town included many artists, even as today.

Beginning in 1896 crowds of tourists from many parts of the world thronged Mill Valley to board the open canopied cars of the Mt. Tamalpais and Muir Woods Railway–eight miles and 281 curves up the mountain to the tavern near the top. Trains on the legendary 'crookedest railroad in the world' stopped running in 1930.

DOWNTOWN MILL VALLEY: Center of the main downtown area is Lytton Square, named in memory of Lytton Barber, first local resident to die in World War I. Buildings on the square and in other business areas were painted in modern hues during an award-winning civic beautification program (1966–1968) sponsored by citizen groups and the Mill Valley Chamber of Commerce.

Lytton Square is the starting point for the famous Dipsea foot race, 6.8 miles over a ridge of Mount Tamalpais to Stinson Beach. The annual race originated in 1905 and is held in late summer or early fall under sponsorship of the Mill Valley Jaycees. In 1972, more than 1,100 runners took part.

The clubhouse of the Mill Valley Outdoor Art Club, West Blithedale and Throckmorton Avenues, was designed by architect Bernard Maybeck and dates from 1905.

Across the street from the Outdoor Art Club is Our Lady of Mt. Carmel Catholic Church, built in 1968, which features a copper-covered spire topped by an 18-foot gold leaf cross, tallest in the county. Architect was Fred Houweling.

El Paseo is a winding passage of shops, offices and restaurants between Throckmorton and Sunnyside Avenues, designed by Gus Costigan in old brick and hand-hewn-lumber motif and opened in 1941.

[34]

At Throckmorton and Miller Avenues is the railway station where trains arrived until late in 1940; at an earlier station, passengers also transferred to the mountain railway. The present building is owned by the city, which in 1954 bought the property and railroad right-of-way along Miller Avenue to Camino Alto and paid for them with coins from parking meters.

Mill Valley Public Library, built in 1966 in the redwoods at 375 Throckmorton, was designed by architects Wurster, Bernardi and Emmons, and won an AIA award. The granite sculpture and benches at the entrance are the work of Mill Valley sculptor Richard O'Hanlon.

JOHN REED'S SAWMILL (State Historical Landmark No. 207): The sawmill built by Reed in 1836 on the bank of Cascade (Old Mill) Creek was the first in Marin County. Its photogenic remains still stand in the midst of tall second-growth redwoods in Old Mill City Park, Cascade Drive off Throckmorton Avenue.

A city-owned area with more recent history is the Mill Valley Golf Course. Dating from 1917 when it opened as a private club, this has been a municipal course since the City of Mill Valley bought the property in 1938, and is said to be Marin's oldest public course. The clubhouse is used as a Center for the Performing Arts to present plays, films and programs.

The Mount Tamalpais Region

Marin's friendly local mountain, Tamalpais, is a landmark seen from many miles around. West Peak is the highest (2,604 feet) but it is East Peak (2,586 feet) and its slopes which, to all but the most unimaginative, depict the legendary Sleeping Maiden of the Mountain.

The name is said to be Coast Miwok Indian: 'Tamal' for bay and 'pais' for land of the mountain. At least in legend, Tamal Indians lived here before the white men came.

Hikers have explored the mountain since before the turn of the century and today there are some 250 miles of trails. On Panoramic Highway at the border of Mount Tamalpais State Park is the Alpine-style Mountain Home Inn, dating from 1912.

MOUNT TAMALPAIS STATE PARK: Established in 1928 with 892 acres after a campaign organized by the Tamalpais Conservation Club, 'Mount Tam's' park now comprises 6,205 acres.

The ranger station and park headquarters are located at Pan Toll–Pan as in panoramic, Toll for the old toll road– where there is also a family campground. Camp Alice Eastwood, named for a pioneer botanist, is for group picnicking and camping (reservations: 388-2070). There are day-use-only picnic areas at Bootjack and East Peak.

It was at East Peak that the trains of the Mt. Tamalpais and Muir Woods Railway arrived during the years 1896–1930. A large tavern stood on the spot.

A short but rocky trail leads to the fire lookout on East Peak where fire-watchers scan the area 24 hours a day during the dry season. There has been a lookout here since 1901, first used to sight ships and since 1921 to watch for fires. The lookout was dedicated in 1937 in memory of Edwin B. Gardner, first warden of the Tamalpais Forest Fire District.

The huge natural bowl of the Mountain Theatre has been the scene of the Mountain Play each year in May since 1913. Many in the audience bring lunch–ranging from a single sandwich to chicken and champagne–and those who are wise also bring cushions for the hard rock seats. The amphitheatre site was donated by William Kent and named in memory of Sidney B. Cushing, president of the Mt. Tamalpais and Muir Woods Railway.

WATERSHED LANDS: Adjoining Mount Tamalpais State Park on the north are some 16,000 acres of watershed lands held by the Marin Municipal Water District.

Most of the watershed area is open for hiking and horseback riding on the trails, fishing in the lakes, and picnicking in six areas (free map and copy of rules available from MMWD office, 220 Nellen Avenue, Corte Madera.)

West Point Inn–where passengers on the Mt. Tamalpais and Muir Woods Railway once transferred to the Bolinas stage and play-goers disembarked to walk on to the Mountain Theatre–is open to hikers as a rest and lunch stop. The building and grounds are leased from the water district by the West Point Club, formed by hiking enthusiasts to preserve the historic 1904 inn.

Other land leased by the district includes that for the U. S. Air Force radar station on West Peak.

Four of the water district's six lakes or reservoirs, set in the forested canyons below Mount Tamalpais, lie along the thread of Lagunitas Creek. Lake Lagunitas spills into Bon Tempe, which spills into Alpine, which spills into Kent; eventually the water flows into Tomales Bay. The district's other two lakes are Phoenix and Nicasio.

MUIR WOODS NATIONAL MONUMENT: In 1907 a water company threatened to condemn a canyon of huge redwoods, cut the trees to finance a dam, and flood the canyon for a reservoir. The move was prevented by William Kent; he bought the property and deeded it to the U. S. Government.

The canyon of redwoods became Muir Woods National Monument, named at Kent's request for his friend, naturalist John Muir. President Theodore Roosevelt established the monument by proclamation in 1908.

It was also Kent who suggested the spur line over which visitors coasted down to the canyon in 'gravity cars' during the days of the Mt. Tamalpais and Muir Woods Railway.

Visitors today drive or hike to Muir Woods. The monument now comprises 503 acres, preserving virgin stands of massive Coast Redwoods (Sequoia Sempervirens), some more than 200 feet tall and centuries old, plus other trees, ferns and wildflowers.

Hundreds of thousands see Muir Woods every year. Leaflets for foreign visitors are printed in seven languages.

There is no picnicking in Muir Woods but a snack bar and souvenir shop are located in the headquarters building.

MUIR BEACH STATE PARK: Muir Beach as a state park dates from 1969, when the 16-acre property was purchased with funds from an anonymous donor plus matching funds from the state.

The park includes part of the rocky portions of the beach, known locally for years for the many sea anemone and other organisms visible at low tide. There is also a large sandy area.

The beach is under the jurisdiction of Mount Tamalpais State Park, and is for day use only.

The adjacent community of Muir Beach dates from the 1890's.

MUIR BEACH OVERLOOK: This nine-acre county park is located 1.3 miles north of Muir Beach off Highway 1; entrance is the same as that to Seacape. Visitors have dramatic views of ocean and rugged coastline from the top platform, or from a promontory approached down a narrow trail with handrails. There are picnic tables in a sheltered area.

The site, acquired by the county in 1960, was used for a coast artillery installation during World War II. Gun emplacements may still be seen. ⮞

Central Marin

The route through what is sometimes called The Valley–Corte Madera and Larkspur, then Kentfield, Ross and San Anselmo in Ross Valley–is an old one for both railway and highway. Passenger trains ran from 1875 to March of 1941. The main road for horse-drawn vehicles and then automobiles went through The Valley until Highway 101 was opened in 1930 on the present alignment.

Yesterday's small settlements are the substantial and pleasant communities of today, with boundaries that are hard to distinguish without the aid of a map. Yet each community has its own special history and character.

Corte Madera

Incorporated 1916; area 4.23 square miles; 1970 population 9,645; post office established 1878, closed 1880, re-opened 1902.

'Corte Madera' is one of Marin's historic names, and there are two theories as to how the name came to be used for the present incorporated town. It may have been because the land grant *Rancho Corte de Madera del Presidio* extended to the southern parts of the town. Or the name may have derived from the fact that *corte madera*, meaning cut wood in Spanish, also was used as the name for the place where the wood was cut; several such places nearby are marked on old maps.

In any event, Corte Madera became the name of the early settlement and of the post office opened in 1878, first in the Valley. But the office closed after two years. When it was re-assigned in 1902 the postmark was 'Adams, California' because the postmaster, Jerry Adams, liked that name. Nobody in town agreed. Two months later, irate citizens succeeded in having the name changed back to Corte Madera.

The 1902 post office was located in Adams's hotel-saloon, first business structure in town. Today, occupied by the Parkside Apartments and Trifles & Treasures, the building still stands at the corner of First Street and Montecito Drive on the Village Square. The post office was moved later to another building on the square and in 1969 to its present location near the Corte Madera civic center complex.

The Village Square was Corte Madera's earliest shopping center, where stores clustered near the railway station. In 1916 the first Town Council persuaded the railroad to help landscape an area near the depot and named it Menke Park in honor of Town Clerk George Menke.

Early Corte Madera's most celebrated resident was Frank M. Pixley, San Francisco city attorney at the time of the Vigilantes, state attorney general, banker, and fiery editor-founder of the long-time magazine *Argonaut*. Owl's Wood, the 191-acre Pixley country estate of the 1880's and early 1890's, today is the site of Chevy Chase Park, the areas around the Village Square, and Corte Madera Hill. A street is named Owlswood and there is a Pixley Avenue.

Another name that survived is Meadowsweet, for a dairy operated 1929–1939. Cows pastured where Madera Gardens and the Corte Madera Shopping Center are today. The milking barn at Meadowsweet Drive and Conow Street was purchased by Mrs. Charlotte Conow and converted to apartments; another remodeled barn is used by the private Meadowsweet School.

Also on Meadowsweet Drive is the new Corte Madera Regional Library, built in 1971 as a joint project of the Town of Corte Madera and County of Marin, and recipient of two 1972 national design awards. Architects were Smith, Barker and Hanssen.

Corte Madera's handsome Town Park once was tidal marsh; its 23 acres were purchased by the town in 1939. In 1952 the Corte Madera Lions Club built a Recreation Center on the edge of the park and deeded it to the town.

When the Town of Corte Madera was a half-century old in 1966, the council commissioned artist Kenneth Potter to paint a mural, depicting historical highlights and characters—one of them Frank M. Pixley—on a wall of the council chambers in the Town Hall.

Corte Madera and its neighbor, Larkspur, are often called Twin Cities. They share schools, recreation programs and a historical society; old-fashioned Fourth of July celebrations are sponsored by the two Chambers of Commerce. ❧

Larkspur

Incorporated 1908; area 3.25 square miles; 1970 population 10,719; post office established 1891.

Larkspur, according to a local story, was named by an English woman, Mrs. C. W. Wright, whose husband laid out the original townsite for a development company in 1887. Mrs. Wright suggested naming the new town for a spring flower she thought was a larkspur–but it was a lupine.

On the 1887 map, most streets were named for trees– magnolia, locust, madrone, a dozen more–but not redwood (a Redwood Avenue came later). But marking a boundary on the map is a 'redwood stump,' one of many left when the giant redwoods were cut and hauled away decades before to account for the area's first history.

A marker placed in 1972 by the Larkspur-Corte Madera Historical Society and City of Larkspur notes 1816 as the earliest known date for shipping redwood logs out of the area; that an official U. S. port was designated in 1846; and a government sawmill operated 1847–1850.

The plaque is located on Magnolia Avenue at Doherty Drive, near the sites of the old sawmill and landings on a finger of Corte Madera Creek. Other historical dates on the marker include 1852 as the year Jonathan Bickerstaff built the first house in Larkspur, at what is now the location of the Niven Company greenhouses.

A second sawmill site in Larkspur is on West Baltimore Avenue just off Magnolia, where the Baltimore and Frederick Mining and Trading Company operated for a short time in 1849. The site is marked by an oak tree with concrete curbing.

Second-growth redwoods still thrive, and one grove of trees is the location of Dolliver City Park at Magnolia and Madrone Avenues. The land was donated by Clarence Burtchael in memory of his mother, Clara Dolliver Burtchael.

Ranching followed the days of lumbering, and when C. W. Wright bought land to lay out the town it was from rancher Patrick King, for whom a street was named.

A landmark in the early-day town was the Hotel Larkspur, built in 1895. Today this is the Blue Rock Inn at 507 Magnolia, still a landmark. The hotel was renamed after it was remodeled in 1911 and faced with blue basalt from a local quarry.

In a redwood grove at 234 Magnolia is a residence built in 1888 by a man named Murphy, now restored as the Lark Creek Inn. Additions and decor match the original Victorian architecture.

Another landmark is Escalle's, 771 Magnolia, once a popular inn selling wine made from grapes grown on nearby hillsides. The present owners have restored the old red brick buildings but they are not open to the public.

A Larkspur tradition for decades was the Saturday night Rosebowl Dance. Named for roses which climbed the first chicken-wire fence, the dances were staged by the Volunteer Fire Department on a half-acre, open-air platform built under the trees and lighted by 3,000 colored bulbs. Average attendance was 2,000 a week. Firemen used proceeds from the dances to build a firehouse and buy equipment which in 1957 they turned over to the city. The first dance on the huge platform was held in 1913 and the last in 1963. Now the Rosebowl Apartments occupy the site at 476 Cane Street.

GREENBRAE AND BON AIR: About half of Greenbrae, on the north side of Sir Francis Drake Boulevard, and most of Bon Air, on the south, are within the Larkspur city limits. Greenbrae was the name of a ranch in the 1870's and Bon Air that of a turn-of-the-century resort hotel. Palm trees mark the hotel site, where Marin General Hospital has been located since 1952, on Bon Air Road.

The Greenbrae turn-off from Highway 101 is the starting point for Sir Francis Drake Boulevard westward on its 42 winding miles to the tip of Point Reyes Peninsula. The route is an old one and was named for Sir Francis Drake after major improvements to the road in 1928–1930.

LARKSPUR FERRY TERMINAL: Ground-breaking ceremonies were held in February 1972 by the Golden Gate Bridge, Highway and Transportation District on its 25-acre Central Marin ferry terminal site at the mouth of Corte Madera Creek in Larkspur. The terminal is scheduled to be operating in 1975. Three new 165-foot, 750-passenger luxury ferryboats will serve this and the Sausalito terminal.

The Larkspur terminal site is adjacent to the Hutchinson Quarry, a Marin landmark since the early 1920's which now is scheduled to be phased out.

Nearby is the site of the Remillard Brick Company, operated from about 1890 to 1915 and producer in its heydey of thousands of bricks annually. Plans were announced in 1972 to preserve the old kilns by turning them into a complex of restaurant, shops, and historical museum. ∽

Kentfield

Kentfield is best known today as a community of large suburban homes and the location of College of Marin. A century ago, this was a busy settlement and important shipping point called Ross Landing for its founder, James Ross.

The settlement's houses, stores, school, hotel and saloon were located in the vicinity of the present College Avenue and Sir Francis Drake Boulevard. Flat-bottomed schooners came up Corte Madera Creek from the bay to load potatoes, bricks, and wood.

When trains started running in 1875 the local station was listed as Tamalpais because, one story has it, residents of the town of Ross objected to the name Ross Landing. The name was changed to Kent, then to Kentwood, and finally to Kentfield. Kentfield Post Office, opened in 1905, became a branch of San Rafael in 1952.

The story of the family which gave the community its permanent name began in 1871 with the arrival of Mr. and Mrs. A. E. Kent and their young son, William. They purchased acreage in Ross Valley and built a large home on what is now Woodland Avenue which is still occupied by members of the Kent family.

Mrs. Kent offered the family estate in 1903 for the annual Sunny Hills Grape Festival; it was held there for 43 years. In 1908 Mrs. Kent donated land on the west side of College Avenue for a recreation area known as the Tamalpais Centre. Most of the land is now in the College of Marin campus. The Tamalpais Centre Woman's Club occupies one acre.

William Kent was elected to Congress in 1910 and served three terms. He wrote the bill creating the National Park Service, passed in 1916, and at home supported the Save-the-Redwoods League and gave land for Muir Woods and Mount Tamalpais State Park.

Streets and a water district lake were named Kent. Land

for Adaline E. Kent School was donated by the family. In 1938, some 800 acres of the Kent estate were subdivided as Kent Woodlands.

COLLEGE OF MARIN: When Marin Junior College ('Marin JC') opened in August, 1926, there were 85 students enrolled for nine courses taught by a faculty of six.

First classes were held in the upstairs rooms of a redwood shingle residence with bay windows. Offices were downstairs. The barn served as a gymnasium.

Across College Avenue was the assembly hall, a large Mission-style building in the former Tamalpais Centre, deeded with most of its land to the new college by the centre's board of directors headed by William Kent. Today this is the location of the college physical education complex.

Marin Junior College grew and expanded with the county. In 1948, the name was changed to College of Marin. Thousands of students have received vocational training, prepared for four-year colleges, and attended adult classes. The campus functions as a county-wide cultural and activity center.

Olney Hall was named for A. C. Olney, first president of the college. The name Harlan Center honors George H. Harlan, Sr., first president of the board of trustees of the district—now the Marin Community College District, which operates both CoM and the new Indian Valley Colleges near Novato.

Today at College of Marin there are: 12 major buildings, with more planned, on 77 acres; a faculty and staff of 171 plus 200 part-time instructors; some 1,200 courses offered; more than 6,500 students in credit classes and another 3,000 in non-credit adult classes. A record number of 619 degrees, Associate in Arts and Associate in Science, were awarded in 1973. ∞

Ross

Incorporated 1908; area 3.5 square miles; 1970 population 2,742; post office established 1887.

When Ross was incorporated it was because residents wanted a town of their own–a small town. Today, Ross is the smallest of Marin's incorporated communities except for Belvedere.

There is no mail delivery in Ross because residents like the idea of picking up their mail at the post office on the town square, called Ross Common. The present post office was built in 1958 on the site of the old railway station.

Before the days of automobiles, horse-drawn rigs provided transportation to and from the station. A late resident who moved to Ross as a boy in 1906 recalled that he was greatly impressed by the fringed buggies and carriages, some with coachmen in livery, which met the late afternoon train from the city. The colorful rigs were parked higgedly-piggedly all over the common to await their owners and drive them home along the tree-lined roads.

Trees were important to the early residents, as they are today. The first Town Council passed an ordinance protecting the trees. Much of the area had been logged off so more trees were planted to provide the shaded roads and lanes–one named Shady Lane–which are still characteristic of Ross.

Albert Dibblee, who built one of the first Ross mansions in the 1870's, is credited with planting many of the trees. His mansion is now gone and his estate, Fernhill, has been subdivided. Part of the estate on Fernhill Road is occupied by the Katharine Branson School, founded in San Rafael in 1916 and moved to Ross six years later.

First the train station and then the town were named Ross for pioneer settler James Ross, Scottish 49'er and former wine merchant. It was Mrs. Ross who donated land in 1881 for Ross Valley's first church, San Anselmo Chapel (Episcopal), which stood on Lagunitas Road opposite the town hall, across Sir Francis Drake Boulevard from the Art & Garden Center. The site.is now a small town park with a marker on a rock in the center.

A four-ton stone bear settled down on the lawn of the town hall in 1972. The bear is the work of the late sculptor Beniamino Bufano and was donated to the town by Jerome Flax.

In 1967 the wooded 25-acre Natalie Coffin Greene Park near Phoenix Lake was given to the Town of Ross in Mrs. Greene's memory by her husband, A. Crawford Greene.

Ross General Hospital, just outside the town boundary, was founded in 1918.

MARIN ART AND GARDEN CENTER: This ten-acre site in Ross is a county showplace, with modern buildings and two that are historic, two outdoor theaters, an imaginative pre-schoolers' playground, and paths winding among the trees, gardens and lawns.

History of the area goes back more than a century to the days of a private estate. In 1946 Mrs. Norman Livermore, with cooperation from half a dozen groups, purchased the property to start development of today's non-profit cultural center.

The main house had been razed in 1931 but the barn was left, and for several decades has been a little theater called The Barn, home of the Ross Valley Players. The unique octagon-shaped tankhouse is now an art-and-garden library named in memory of artist-teacher Jose Moya del Pino.

Visitors may see the center every day from 9 to 5. Open at certain hours during the week (information: 454-5597) are the Frances Young Gallery, Decorations Guild showroom, Laurel House Antiques, Magnolia Tea Room and Garden Path Shop, as well as the center office where inquiries may be made about classes, nature tours, and other activities.

Special events include an annual festival over the Fourth of July to replace the Art and Garden Fair held at the center 1946–1970, the last 20 years as Marin's official county fair.

A serpentine brick wall was dedicated in 1969 to the memory of Mrs. Livermore (1884–1968). ✍

San Anselmo

Incorporated 1907; area 2.6 square miles; 1970 population 13,031; post office established 1892.

Now Marin's third largest incorporated community, San Anselmo once was a railroad junction known by that name with a capital 'J.' It was the place where the North Pacific Coast Railroad tracks from Ross and points south, to Fairfax and points west, crossed the line to San Rafael.

'Junction' was used only nine years, 1875–1884. After that the trains continued to come through but the station was known by the more pleasing name of San Anselmo. Today, with the trains gone for more than three decades, the distinction as a major crossroads remains, and San Anselmo is sometimes called the Hub of Marin.

The name San Anselmo appears to have derived from the lengthy full title of an 1840 Mexican land grant, *Rancho Punta de Quintin Corte del Madera La Laguna y Cañada de San Anselmo* (Quintin Point, Wood-Cutting Place, the Lake and Valley of Saint Anselm). About half of the present Town of San Anselmo is in this grant and the remainder on the north in *Rancho Cañada de Herrera* (Valley of the Blacksmith). The name Camino de Herrera recalls the latter rancho and another avenue, Sais, is named for the man who received the grant in 1839, Domingo Saís (Saez).

Today's suburban community and business center was a recreation area at the turn of the century. Arriving by train, families camped on the creek in what is now downtown San Anselmo. Summer homes and then permanent residences were built, one of them by James Tunstead, county sheriff 1875–1880 and donor of land in 1911 for the town hall and firehouse at San Anselmo and Tunstead Avenues.

After the 1906 earthquake, growth accelerated. Incorporation came when residents resisted an annexation threat from San Rafael. They wanted to control their own town, and especially wanted to keep out saloons such as San Rafael had in abundance. There is said to have been only one non-dry place in town–the Tea Pot, where the tea was whiskey.

San Anselmo's well-known natural landmark, Red Hill, gave its name to a street, a school and the newest shopping center. Red Hill Shopping Center's location on Sir Francis Drake Boulevard was the site of the Grape Festival, 1949–1965. Now held at the county fairgrounds, the festival is a traditional benefit for Sunny Hills, an orphanage founded in 1895 and today a residential treatment center for emotionally disturbed adolescents. The institution was moved from San Rafael to San Anselmo in 1900 and now occupies a complex of buildings on Sunny Hills Drive.

Located on a three-acre former private estate at 237 Crescent Road is an unusual town park: Robson-Harrington. The large house, built about 1910, is surrounded by gardens. It is now used as a community center.

SAN FRANCISCO THEOLOGICAL SEMINARY: This Presbyterian seminary was founded in San Francisco in 1871 and moved in 1892 to San Anselmo, where railroad magnate A. W. Foster had donated land. The ivy-covered towers of the two original buildings, Scott and Montgomery Halls, are still landmarks on Seminary Hill. Geneva Hall was built in 1952 on the crown of the hill.

Newest building (1971) on the 24-acre campus is the Lloyd Education Center, Austin Avenue and Kensington Road. Scott Hall is now used by the School of Arts and Sciences, a private high school.

When classes started in 1871 there were four seminarians. 1973 enrollment totaled 631 full-time and part-time students, and 99 degrees were granted.

The seminary is a graduate theological school controlled by the General Assembly of the United Presbyterian Church in the U. S. A. Doctoral degrees are granted in conjunction with the Graduate Theological Union, Berkeley, an inter-denominational group of seminaries in which the San Anselmo school is a participant. Seminarians live and attend classes both in San Anselmo and Berkeley.

SLEEPY HOLLOW: The suburban community adjacent to incorporated San Anselmo once was the location of a dairy ranch operated by Harvey B. Butterfield, then by Richard M. Hotaling and later, until 1925, by Sigmund K. Herzog. The dairy buildings of the Sleepy Hollow Ranch became the Sleepy Hollow Stables at 1251 Butterfield Road. In 1971 they were torn down and replaced by homes.

Hotaling built a mansion at the end of Butterfield Road which was remodeled in the late 1920's as the clubhouse for the Sleepy Hollow Golf Club. The mansion burned down in 1957. Today its wide steps and foundations are landmarks at the entrance to San Domenico School for Girls, dedicated in 1966.

It was probably Hotaling who planted the poplar and eucalyptus trees which still line Butterfield Road for the last mile and a half. ✣

Fairfax

Incorporated 1931; area 1.7 square miles; 1970 population 7,661; post office established 1910.

Fairfax was named for Charles Snowden Fairfax, member of a prominent Virginia family whose founders had brought along a 17th century title when they emigrated from England to Colonial America. Officially, Charles was Lord Fairfax, 10th Baron of Cameron, but he disdained noble trappings and refused to claim the title. (Today, according to *Who's Who*, the 14th Lord Fairfax–Nicholas, great-great nephew of Charles–lives in England.)

Charles Fairfax arrived in California in 1849 and soon entered state politics. He was a colorful character of post-Gold Rush times, known for his attire (brown velvet coat, shirt with lace ruffles) and gentlemanly conduct, whether taking part in political affairs, gambling or drinking. In 1865–1867 he was a Marin County supervisor.

When Fairfax married in 1855 he received as a wedding gift 32 acres on Cascade Creek in what is now the Town of Fairfax. He built a home for his bride that was the scene of lavish entertaining–he is said to have cooled his champagne in the creek–and in 1861 of the state's last political duel. After Fairfax died in 1869 the estate was sold by his widow.

In later years the property was used for Pastori's, a famous Italian restaurant; The Emporium Country Club; and a recreation area, the Marin Town and Country Club. The Fairfax home site is a state historical landmark.

Fairfax was widely known as a recreation spot before it became the residential community of today. Every weekend, crowds poured in on special trains. The original picnic grounds extended over much of the present downtown area.

In the early 1920's the Fairfax Volunteer Fire Department bought part of the picnic grounds, Fairfax Park, and added a pavilion in which big dances and other events were held.

The Marin Music Chest's first concert in 1934 took place there.

After incorporation the firemen turned the park over to the Town of Fairfax. Today it is a town park and the pavilion is a recreation center.

A local novelty from 1913 to 1929 was the Fairfax Funicular, 500 feet up the hill on a wooden trestle to Fairfax Manor subdivision. Fare on the one cable car was five cents. A line of power poles from Sequoia Road to Scenic Road still marks the spot.

To Fairfax visitors, the location of Manor is often a mystery. This was a tiny 1913 subdivision north of the downtown area which has kept the name. There was a Manor post office, 1915–1953. Manor was the last stop in town during the days of the trains. Today Oak Tree Lane in Manor, off Sir Francis Drake Boulevard, is the end of the line for the Golden Gate Transit buses.

SITE OF LORD FAIRFAX HOME (State Historical Landmark No. 679): A marker was placed in 1960 at the site of the Fairfax estate, Bird's Nest Glen, located at the end of Pastori Avenue off Sir Francis Drake Boulevard. The Fairfax home burned in 1911 and a new building, now the office of the Marin Town and Country Club, was constructed on the old foundation.

DEER PARK: This 53-acre county park in the northern edge of the Marin Municipal Water District lands has been leased (at $1 per year) from the district by the county since 1968. Deer Park School is in the park, and access to both is from Bolinas Road over Porteous Avenue.

There are picnic tables, but the park's main feature is the opportunity for nature walks through meadows and wooded lanes. Ridge Trail takes off from the park to connect with the network of trails over Mount Tamalpais.

Deer Park Subdivision, nearby, was a 1907 residential development. The restaurant named Deer Park Villa at 367 Bolinas Road dates from 1922.

WHITE'S HILL: The smoothly-paved road over White's Hill out of Fairfax, even with its steep grade, is no problem for today's automobiles. A century and more ago the hill was a major challenge for travelers in buggies and wagons. They demanded a 'good road' and, when it was built in 1865, were elated that two teams of horses could pass.

Trains went through the hill in tunnels, 1875–1933.

White's Hill was named for an early rancher whose first name may have been Lorenzo.

OPEN SPACE–CAMP AREAS: Almost 1,000 acres in the hills northwest of Fairfax are preserved as open space and enjoyed by thousands of youngsters.

Some 800 acres of primitive camping area are included in Camp Tamarancho, operated by Marin Council of the Boy Scouts of America. The land was purchased in 1943 with funds from an anonymous donor.

Adjoining Tamarancho are nearly 200 acres of the Bothin Youth Center, operated by the San Francisco Bay Girl Scout Council and named for the late Henry E. Bothin of Ross, land owner and philanthropist.

Bothin Youth Center has two sections, Camp Arequipa and Bothin Manor. Arequipa (an ancient Peruvian Indian word for place of rest) was the site of a tuberculosis sanatorium for women, 1911–1957. A pottery was operated during its early years, with patients decorating the earthenware pieces. Today these are collector's items and Arequipa Pottery is represented in the Smithsonian Institution, Washington, D.C., and in the Oakland Museum.

The second section of the Girl Scout area, Bothin Manor, is on the site of Hill Farm convalescent home for children, operated from 1905 until the 1940's. ∂∞

[56]

The San Geronimo Valley

WOODACRE: Post Office established 1925

SAN GERONIMO: Post Office established 1895

FOREST KNOLLS: Post Office established 1916

LAGUNITAS: Post Office established 1906

Joseph Warren Revere bought *Rancho Cañada de San Geronimo* (Valley of Saint Jerome) in 1846 and later described it as 'one of the loveliest valleys in California.' It still is.

Revere, whose grandfather, Paul, was the celebrated silversmith and 1775 midnight rider, is one of several famous figures in the valley's past. He was the U. S. Navy lieutenant who pulled down the Bear Flag at Sonoma on July 9, 1846, and raised the Stars and Stripes to signal the end of the Bear Flag Revolt and the beginning of United States possession of California. Revere bought the valley of San Geronimo later that same year, and tried ranching. But he soon sold out and departed.

In 1873, Adolph Mailliard (MY-ard) arrived with his family. He was the son of Louis Mailliard, illegitimate son of Joseph Bonaparte, Emperor Napoleon's older brother. Once king of Naples and then of Spain, Joseph had lived in exile in Bordentown, New Jersey, with Louis as confidential secretary, and Adolph was born there. Adolph and his family left their villa near the former 'royal' estate to come to California.

On more than 6,000 acres of the San Geronimo Valley, Adolph Mailliard established three dairy ranches and built a mansion in what is now Woodacre. The mansion with its 18 rooms and 12 fireplaces saw many visitors including Mrs. Mailliard's sister, Julia Ward Howe, the famous abolitionist and author of 'The Battle Hymn of the Republic.'

Another visitor was a man by the name of Alexander Graham Bell, who is said to have demonstrated a new-fangled invention with the aid of barbed wire between the house and barn.

A giant rock in a meadow near the mansion was a favorite family retreat. Today this is called Castle Rock and the headquarters of the Marin County Fire Department are located next to it on Castle Rock Avenue in Woodacre.

On hunting trips in the hills the Mailliard sons, John (grandfather of Congressman William S. Mailliard) and Joseph collected birds' nests and eggs. This began a life-long hobby, and their collection, together with field notes from bird banding and other expeditions, is now at the California Academy of Sciences in San Francisco.

Both Mr. and Mrs. Mailliard died in the 1890's at their ranch home, and in 1912 their children sold the family property. Summer home tracts were subdivided by the Lagunitas Development Company at San Geronimo and Lagunitas, both early settlements, and at new areas named Woodacre and Forest Knolls.

At Woodacre, the Mailliard mansion became Woodacre Lodge and then the clubhouse of the Woodacre Improvement Club. In 1958 the old mansion burned down and a new clubhouse was built. Today this is the clubhouse of the San Geronimo Valley Swim and Tennis Club, successor to the Improvement Club.

[58]

The trains that had started running through the valley in 1875 ceased operating in 1933, and all the stations except one have since disappeared. The exception is San Geronimo Station, now being restored by a group of valley residents as a 19th century railway station-museum. The station is located on San Geronimo Valley Road adjacent to the Community Presbyterian Church.

Nearby is the Roy Ranch home, built during the 1880's, which will be converted into a pro shop for the San Geronimo National Racquet Club. The club will be operated in conjunction with the adjacent San Geronimo National Golf Club which opened in 1965.

SAMUEL P. TAYLOR STATE PARK (State Historical Landmark No. 552): This 2,576-acre park is named for Samuel Penfield Taylor, a 49'er from New York who in 1856 built the Pacific Coast's first paper mill on the banks of what is now called Paper Mill Creek.

The Pioneer Paper Mill, using water power and then steam, became a big operation. At its peak, the production was five tons of paper a day—from old rags and jute, not timber. But the business failed in 1893 and the buildings burned down in 1915.

Today all to be seen at the site, 1.2 miles from the main gate, are some of the rough concrete foundations with huge steel bolts protruding and a few iron straps or hoops from the 30-inch redwood pipe that once took water to the mill's waterwheel.

The mill site is a state historical landmark. A marker was placed in 1956.

Taylor's paper mill lasted less than 40 years but a custom he started, vacationing in the redwoods in the vicinity of the mill, lasts to this day. Taylor welcomed visitors when they arrived on the narrow-gauge railroad starting in 1875; they could pitch their tents on the banks of the creek or stay at his big resort hotel.

The trains stopped running in 1933, and today visitors driving or walking to the mill site on the west side of the creek follow a road built where the tracks used to be. The hotel was located in what is now the main picnic area near park headquarters.

The state park was created in 1945 after five years of campaigning by the Marin Conservation League.

There are campsites and picnic areas along Paper Mill Creek, a swimming hole made by damming the creek, and miles of trails. One of the trails leads to Barnabe Mountain, named for the Taylor children's pet white mule which grazed there. Barnabe was an Army mule said to have been brought across the plains with Captain John C. Fremont's men. He was buried on his mountain, but no one knows where.

The fire lookout on Barnabe Peak was dedicated in 1940 to Fred W. Dickson, valley rancher who donated the land.

Campsite reservations are made through Ticketron, Inc. For day use the park is open from 8 A.M. to 9 P.M.

History-minded visitors may take the 'history walk' with a park ranger, visiting the old papermill site among other places and seeing a collection of buttons cut from old rags from which paper was made by Samuel P. Taylor more than a century ago.

TOCALOMA: This was a ranching center with its own post office, 1891–1919, and its own school. Tocaloma also was a stop on the railroad with a hotel, the Bertrand House, that was a sportsmen's favorite. The hotel burned down in 1917 and a former opera singer named Caesar Ronchi built a tavern said to have been frequented by San Francisco literati and/or Prohibition-time gangland types. According to another story, Caesar's Salad originated at the tavern.

The old tavern building, now with a No Trespassing sign, may still be seen. The site is off Sir Francis Drake Boulevard about a mile and a half north of Samuel P. Taylor Park.

The name Tocaloma is said to be of Indian origin; the creek was once known as the Tokelalume.

Another name on the highway dating from railroad days is Jewell, just north of Taylor Park, for rancher Omar Jewell, who arrived in the early 1860's. ∞

Nicasio

Post Office established 1871

Rich in history, this area still retains a flavor of the past. 'A priceless vignette of Early California' is the way the village of Nicasio and the ranching country which surrounds it are described in a 1970 study by the Marin County Planning Department.

Today's village with its open square must look much the same as it did a century ago—although it was bigger and busier then, with two stores, a church, post office, livery stable, saloons and other buildings around the square, and a school nearby. Stagecoaches brought guests to the three-story Nicasio Hotel.

The open village square dates from 1863, when it was intended for a new county courthouse; residents thought Nicasio should be the county seat. An election was held and San Rafael won, but the square survived.

The church and the school have been preserved and are among Marin's best-known historical landmarks. Our Lady of Loretto Catholic Church, dedicated in 1867, is still in use for Sunday masses. A marker was placed in 1965 by the Native Sons and Daughters of the Golden West.

Old Nicasio School, around the corner from the village square on the Nicasio-San Geromino Road, was built in 1871 and used for classes until a new school was opened in 1949. The old school is now a private residence.

Fire destroyed the Nicasio Hotel in 1940 but in its place facing the open square is Rancho Nicasio, a restaurant-bar-grocery-post office-realty office and the only business place in town. Headquarters of the Volunteer Fire Department are next door.

The Druids Hall on the square, built in 1933 to replace an 1885 hall which burned down, is the center of activity for Nicasio Grove of the Druids Lodge and also is used for meetings of community groups. Adjacent to the hall is a century-old building that once was a butcher shop.

Nicasio was part of one of Marin's biggest land grants, nearly 57,000 acres named *Rancho Nicasio* (probably for Saint Nicasius, or for an Indian convert who took that name). In 1855 some 31,000 acres of the rancho were owned by Henry W. Halleck, prominent lawyer and one of the authors of the state constitution, who became general-in-chief of the Union Armies during the Civil War. Halleck hunted and fished in Nicasio Valley and had a cabin, now gone, on the creek named for him. The future general provided 30 acres for Indians from Mission San Rafael who had congregated in the valley. They ended their days there.

NICASIO POINT NATURE PRESERVE: The 22-acre county preserve juts out into Nicasio Lake to the dam at the southern end. It is undeveloped, and has no public access. The land was donated in 1968 by William Field of Nicasio.

Nicasio Lake, completed in 1960 on the floor of the valley, is the newest and biggest of Marin Municipal Water District's reservoirs. The district holds some 2,000 acres in this area.

In 1972 the district, Boy Scouts and the Marin County Board of Realtors began a program to plant thousands of native trees and shrubs around Nicasio Lake. ॐ

San Quentin Peninsula

An Indian named Quintin, one of the leaders in the last resistance put up by Marin Indians against their white conquerors, was captured here by Mexican soldiers in 1824 after fleeing south from the Marin Islands where Chief Marin had taken refuge (page 77).

Quintin was later released and, like Chief Marin, worked on boats crossing the bay. The land grant *Rancho Punta de Quintin* was named for him; it isn't clear as to how the spelling was later changed to Quentin or the San for Saint was added.

The rancho was acquired by Benjamin R. Buckelew, who envisoned a metropolis he called 'Marin City' to replace his former dream of a 'California City' on the Tiburon Peninsula (page 32). Instead of a city, there was a prison; Buckelew sold the state the first 20 acres in 1852.

SAN QUENTIN PRISON: In July of 1852 the old brig *Waban* was towed to San Quentin Point with the first prisoners. From then on, the prison's tumultous history was one of politics, scandals, controversy, violence, fires, riots, executions and escapes, as well as innovations and reform. At one time more than 5,000 inmates were held. They included women prisoners until the fall of 1933.

In the village called San Quentin, where the main prison gates are located at the end of San Quentin Street, some of the old wooden buildings have false fronts which add a frontier look. Prisoners' work is sold in the San Quentin Handicraft Shop near the gates, open to the public daily.

San Quentin Post Office dates from 1859.

San Quentin Point has been a transportation terminal since the 1860's when Petaluma River steamers stopped there to transfer passengers to stagecoaches for San Rafael. Trains replaced the stages, and the point served as a rail and ferry terminal until 1884.

San Quentin Point became the Marin terminal for the Richmond-San Rafael auto ferries in 1916. Ferryboats ran until the present bridge was opened over the same route across San Francisco Bay.

RICHMOND-SAN RAFAEL BRIDGE. Constructed by the state beginning in 1953, the bridge was dedicated August 31, 1956. The upper deck was opened to traffic the next day and a year later the lower deck also was in use.

Total length of the toll bridge and approaches is 5½ miles; of the bridge proper, four miles. The two main cantilever-type spans are 1,000 feet long and the highest tower is 325 feet above the water.

Pedestrians and bicyclists are not permitted. ∂∞

San Rafael

Incorporated 1874; area 20.87 square miles; 1973 population 43,800; post office established 1851.

San Rafael is not only the county seat of Marin and its principal city, but the oldest: this is where the county started. Coast Miwok Indians were the sole inhabitants of the land now known as Marin when Mission San Rafael Arcangel was founded in 1817.

With the arrival of white settlers, a half-dozen houses clustered in the vicinity of the mission. San Rafael's first town lots were laid out in 1850 along numbered and lettered streets near the mission compound. The site where the mission stood, now the location of a mission replica and St. Raphael's Catholic Church, is still the center of downtown San Rafael.

Mission San Rafael was founded as a sanitarium for Indians from Mission Dolores in San Francisco and named for Saint Raphael, the angel of bodily healing. First an *asistencia* (branch) of Dolores, San Rafael became a full mission in 1823–next-to-last in the chain of 21 and last to be established while the Spanish ruled California.

Just how the mission looked is puzzling to historians. No painting or sketch of the building while it stood has been found, and pictures done later from memory or imagination vary in detail. It is known that the two-story chapel and wing of one story formed an L-shape and were of simple adobe construction, with no embellishments such as the 'star windows' in the present replica. The chapel was on the approximate site of St. Raphael's rectory, facing east.

Red tiles for the mission roof were made by Indian converts, who lived in adobe huts on the slope between the present Fifth Avenue and Fourth Street. Indians also helped the mission priests to plant the orchards and vineyards which covered an area bordered by today's Lootens Place and Lincoln Avenue between Third Street and Fifth Avenue.

The legendary figures Chief Marin and Quintin (pages 77 and 63) are said to have been among the Indians baptized at the mission.

San Rafael Mission was one of the first to be taken over in 1834 when all of the missions were secularized (transferred from church to state) and their lands began to be divided into private ranchos. In 1861, San Rafael's mission was torn down to salvage its hand-hewn redwood beams.

Meanwhile, in 1850, Marin had become one of the original 27 counties in the new State of California, with San Rafael as county seat—and the crumbling mission building lasted long enough to serve as the first county courthouse.

The county offices and court were moved in 1853 to a two-story adobe built by Timothy (Don Timoteo) Murphy at Fourth and C Streets, now the location of the Marin Title Guaranty Company. The Murphy adobe was used until a stately new courthouse was finished in 1873.

Murphy, a giant Irishman known for his hospitality to travelers and his kindness to the Indians, was major domo of the mission after secularization and then *alcalde* (magistrate) of the pueblo of San Rafael. In 1844 the Mexican government granted him nearly 22,000 acres of former mission land: *Rancho San Pedro, Santa Margarita y Las Gallinas* (Saint Peter, Saint Margaret and the Hens, or water-fowl). The rancho included the northeastern part of San Rafael proper and stretched north to the present Northgate, Terra Linda, Marinwood and Lucas Valley, as well as east to San Pedro Point. The colorful Don Timoteo died in 1853.

During the town's earliest years, travelers arrived on dirt trails or by boat up San Rafael Creek from the bay. The town grew as transportation became easier; first stage-coaches, then trains starting in 1870.

San Rafael's residents voted to incorporate four years after the coming of the railroad. For their initial meetings, town officials used a room over a saloon at Short's Hall, Fourth and C Streets, where the Reynolds-Johnson Building is now located.

By the 1880's there was an opera house named Gordon's at the present 1333 Fourth Street, now stores and offices with apartments above; and there were elegant Victorian houses with wide lawns. The town's leading citizens owned large estates and showplace mansions. Of the latter, some survived.

Maple Lawn, the John F. Boyd mansion at 1312 Mission Avenue, was inherited by his explorer daughter, Louise A. Boyd, and today is the San Rafael Elks Club.

The Dollar mansion at 1408 Mission Avenue, built in the late 1870's and purchased in 1907 by steamship magnate Captain Robert Dollar, was saved from demolition by a citizens' group incorporated as Marin Heritage. In 1972, the Dollar Estate was listed on the National Register of Historic Places.

A mansion built around 1870 by banker M. J. O'Connor at Fifth and Cottage Avenues was purchased by A. W. Foster, donated in 1892 to the Tamalpais Military Academy, and named Foster Hall. Tamalpais Academy later became San Rafael Military Academy, which closed in 1971; a private high school, the Marin Academy, replaced it.

Two estates, A. W. Foster's Fairhills and Alexander Forbes's Culloden Park, left their names with present-day residential areas.

In addition to the old mansions, historic buildings include the clubhouse of the San Rafael Improvement Club at Fifth Avenue and H Street, the former Victor Building at the 1915 Panama Pacific Exposition in San Francisco; and St. Paul's Episcopal Church. Built in 1869 at Fourth and E Streets, the church building was moved in 1924 to the present site on Court Street. The wooden exterior has been covered with stucco but the beautiful interior with its stained glass windows is still essentially the same.

Recalling San Rafael's days as a resort city are the stone gate posts at the entrance to Rafael Drive at Belle Avenue. Only the posts were left when the big and luxurious Hotel Rafael burned in 1928 after standing only 40 years.

Grand is still the name of a tree-lined avenue in a major subdivision developed by William T. Coleman, millionaire San Francisco merchant and Vigilante leader. In 1887 he sold land to the Dominican Sisters, and today the vicinity of their college is called the Dominican area; but a street and a school were named for Coleman. Coleman's country home was in San Rafael, located, according to some accounts, at the present 1130 Mission Avenue.

San Rafael was a railroad center for a century. In 1971 Northwestern Pacific closed its local facilities and left the Tamalpais Avenue depot and offices vacant—but not for long. The Marin Senior Coordinating Council leased the building, and, with major help from the Marin Soroptimist Club, refurbished the old waiting room as a county-wide senior center named the Whistlestop. Part of the building is occupied by the Marin General Hospital Volunteers' Thrift Shop.

The 1873 courthouse was used until the last of the county offices and courts moved to the new Civic Center in 1969. On May 25, 1971, fire destroyed the empty courthouse. The 1958 annex on Fifth Avenue survived, only to be scheduled for demolition to clear the old courthouse square for an office building complex.

PIONEER PARKS: Land for several San Rafael parks was given to the city by pioneer residents. Boyd Park, Mission Avenue and B Street, was dedicated in 1905 on land donated by Mr. and Mrs. John F. Boyd. Captain Robert Dollar added land in 1923 and the park's scenic drive is named for him.

Gerstle Park at San Rafael Avenue and Clark Street was a gift in 1930 from the family of Mr. and Mrs. Lewis Gerstle. Land for Albert Park at B and Treanor Streets was donated by Jacob Albert in 1937. Albert also gave land and funds for Scout Hall, the Marin Boy Scout Council building at Second and A Streets.

MISSION SAN RAFAEL REPLICA (State Historical Landmark No. 220): Building of the replica in 1949 with funds from the Hearst Foundation followed a four-year campaign by the Marin County Historical Society.

The replica consists of two wings, one a chapel in the style and spirit of the old mission, used for weddings and special services, and the other a museum-gift shop. Both are open to visitors from 11 A.M. to 4 P.M. weekdays and from 10 A.M. to 4 P.M. Sundays.

Three of the mission's original four bells, one of them found in 1972 in San Diego County, hang just outside the chapel entrance. The fourth bell is at the side on Fifth Avenue.

A pear tree also at the side of the chapel on Fifth Avenue was donated by San Rafael nurseryman Karl Untermann, who grew it from a graft taken from one of the last trees in the mission orchards.

San Rafael Mission was designated a state historical landmark in 1934.

MARIN COUNTY HISTORICAL SOCIETY MUSEUM: Hundreds of items and photos depicting the history of Marin are on display in the museum, located at Mission Avenue and B Street on the edge of Boyd Park.

At the entrance is a huge iron kettle used in the 1840's at Rancho Olompali north of Novato for 'trying' tallow from cattle, elk and deer. In 1846 the kettle is said to have served as a stew pot for soldiers.

Exhibits include Indian artifacts, Sir Francis Drake memorabilia, old maps and newspapers, and early-day household items. The late Roy D. Graves, historian and former museum curator, provided many of the historical photos from his collection of more than 40,000 pictures now in the Bancroft Library, U.C., Berkeley.

The Victorian structure occupied by the museum was built in the late 1870's as a guest lodge for Maple Lawn, the nearby Boyd mansion now the Elks Club. Three of the original eight marble fireplaces may still be seen in the museum building.

The historical society, founded in 1935, opens the museum to visitors from 2 to 5 P.M. Wednesday, Saturday and Sunday. Guided tours may be arranged.

LOUISE A. BOYD MARIN MUSEUM OF SCIENCE: Visitors of all ages (from 3 up) learn about nature at this museum at 76 Albert Park Lane. Outdoors there is a small zoo, and indoors are exhibits including dioramas of wildlife and a Coast Miwok Indian village. A gift shop has nature books available plus information on classes, lectures and field trips.

Boyd Museum has been a refuge for hundreds of wild animals found abandoned or injured. Staff members take wildlife exhibits and nature instruction to the county's schools.

The museum building is the former parish hall of St. Paul's Episcopal Church, moved to the site as a contribution from the San Rafael Optimist Club.

Opened in 1955, the museum was named for Louise Arner Boyd, noted explorer and native of San Rafael. Miss Boyd made eight Arctic expeditions and was honored by the U.S. and other governments and by geographical societies. She died in 1972 at the age of 84.

The museum is open to visitors from 10 A.M. to 5 P.M. Tuesday through Saturday and from 12 noon to 5 P.M. Sundays.

DOMINICAN COLLEGE OF SAN RAFAEL: Today's four-year college and graduate school began as a convent and school for girls opened by the Dominican Sisters in 1889. Built first was the massive four-story Convent of redwood, now used for a chapel, sisters' residence, parlor for visitors, and offices. It is still a landmark on Grand Avenue.

The 21 buildings on the 100-acre, tree-studded campus include two other reminders of the elegant 1880's: Meadowlands, the former country home of M. H. DeYoung, and Edgehill, the William Babcock mansion. Both are residence halls.

In 1915 the sisters added a women's college to their elementary and high school departments. The co-educational graduate school dates from 1950; undergraduates have included men students since the fall of 1971.

Dominican offers majors in 22 fields with emphasis on the liberal arts. Enrollment in 1973 was approximately 1,000, including part-time students, and 133 degrees were conferred. ❧

Puerto Suello Hill to Civic Center

The *Puerto Suello* (mountain pass) is an old and scenic gateway between San Rafael proper and the areas immediately north. Highway 101 stretches over Puerto Suello Hill, with a view from the top of miles of rolling hills that are sunbleached in summer, green in winter.

MARIN COUNTY CIVIC CENTER: Marin's most celebrated building, or complex of buildings, is located on a 140-acre site on North San Pedro Road off Highway 101, 2½ miles north of the courthouse it replaced. Designed by world-famous architect Frank Lloyd Wright, the Civic Center has been widely acclaimed, criticized, written about, photographed, and toured by visitors from many states and foreign countries.

Wright designed the two main horizontal buildings–together 1,550 feet long–to bridge four knolls, with wide arches over the entrance roadways. With completion of these two huge buildings, most of the county offices and all of its law courts and agencies, including the sheriff's office and county jail, were combined under one sky-blue roof measuring some four acres.

The Administration Building was dedicated October 13, 1962. It is 700 feet long and contains 140,000 square feet.

Total cost, including furnishings and landscaping, was $5.1 million. The building's 172-foot-high golden aluminum spire conceals a smoke stack to vent the cooling system. On the top floor under the dome is the main Marin County Free Library.

The Hall of Justice, attached to the north end of the Administration Building, was dedicated December 13, 1969. It is 850 feet long and contains 297,000 square feet. Cost for complete development was $11.5 million. One of the building's design features is its round courtrooms.

A gallery on the first floor of the Hall of Justice adjacent to the Administration Building, as well as the foyer of the Board of Supervisors' chambers, are used for exhibits by the Marin Museum Association.

Third major structure on the Civic Center site, the Marin Veterans Memorial, opened September 25, 1971. This $3.5 million building features luxurious appointments and controlled acoustics. A theater for 800 and an adjacent exhibit hall are divided by a partition which can be moved to provide some 1,200 more seats for the theater.

The Veterans Memorial is the scene of concerts including those of the Marin Symphony, Marin Civic Ballet and Marin Music Chest, performances sponsored by the Marin Concert Association and Actors' Playhouse of Marin, and a wide variety of other events.

In 1971, the 80-acre county fairgrounds adjacent to the Veterans Memorial were used for the first time as the site of the Marin County Fair.

Standing near the Veterans Memorial is the bronze 'doughboy' statue, World War I memorial moved from its former location in front of the old courthouse in downtown San Rafael.

The Civic Center grounds and county fairgrounds, including the lagoon in front of the Veterans Memorial, are part of the county park system. ∂∞

To San Pedro Point and Back

One of Marin's most scenic and varied drives is around the big peninsula encircled by a road called San Pedro on the north and Point San Pedro on the south. The ten-mile road from Civic Center Drive to Marina Boulevard on the opposite side of the peninsula links the new (the Civic Center, residential areas, a golf course, yacht harbors on San Rafael Canal) with the very old (China Camp) plus a county beach and brickyard. Along the way are stretches of open marsh and shoreline.

The name of McNear has long been associated with the eastern end of the peninsula. John A. McNear envisioned steamers landing at the point and homes served by a railroad. The dream died in 1906 but work had started on the railroad, and the combination of cuts made in the hills for tracks and the name of a local rancher, Thomas Peacock, is said to have provided the name Peacock Gap for the present residential area and golf-and-country club.

John McNear's son, Erskine B. McNear, Sr., built a brick home now on the property of the Church of the Redeemer (Episcopal) at 121 Knight Drive in Glenwood.

McNear's Brickyard has been a family enterprise since 1898. The high smokestacks are still there but no longer used.

SANTA VENETIA: As planned by real estate promoter Mabry McMahan in 1914, Santa Venetia was to have Venetian-style buildings including a clubhouse built like a palace, a plush hotel, miles of bridle paths, homes along a three-mile canal, and gondolas imported from Venice. Work was started on concrete levees.

McMahan's grandiose scheme was killed by the post-World War I depression. Piles of concrete from his levees are all that remain. Today, McMahan probably would be pleased that the suburban community with frontage on the South Fork of Las Gallinas Creek is still called Santa Venetia and that the world-famous Marin County Civic Center is nearby.

JOHN F. McINNIS PARK: Marin county began acquiring land in 1972 for this regional park on San Pablo Bay at the mouth of Las Gallinas Creek. On 450 acres (290 land, 160 tidelands) of the former Smith Dairy Ranch, the Park will combine preservation of marsh, delta and open space with a recreational complex including a swim and tennis center.

CHINA CAMP: Ramshackle, photogenic old buildings with narrow piers threading out into the water are all that is left of a prosperous settlement of a century ago. At one time in the 1870's as many as 10,000 Chinese are said to have lived here.

Using Chinese junks and later motor launches, fisherman netted the tiny bay shrimps and brought them ashore for cooking, grading and packing. New netting methods were enforced in 1910 and China Camp's population dwindled, but commercial shrimp fishing continued on a smaller scale. Today there are few shrimp left but sports fishermen rent boats to find large fish in the bay.

Rat Rock off China Camp has been owned by the county since 1965.

McNEAR'S BEACH COUNTY PARK: This 52-acre park with half a mile of shoreline on San Pablo Bay opened in 1970. It offers lawn and picnic areas, a swimming pool, playground and tennis courts, plus views of miles of open water.

McNear's Beach, originally operated by members of the McNear family, was popular with Marin residents for several decades beginning in the early 1930's.

THE ISLANDS OF MARIN: A legendary episode in county history took place on the Marin Islands off Point San Pedro near the mouth of San Rafael Creek. The islands are said to have provided refuge for the Indian warrior later called Chief Marin when he and a group of other Indians fought Mexican soldiers in 1824.

Chief Marin's friend Quintin fled south and was captured (page 63), as was Marin two years later. Both were released and worked as ferrymen on the bay. Legend says that the chief was called *El Marinero* in Spanish for mariner or sailor, with Marin as an abbreviation, and that the islands and the county were named for him.

The two small, bare islands known as the Sisters off Point San Pedro have two Brothers named East and West off Richmond in Contra Costa County. A lighthouse built on the East Brother in 1874 was automated in 1969.

The boundaries of Marin, San Francisco and Contra Costa Counties meet at Red Rock, just south of the Richmond-San Rafael Bridge. Stories about Red Rock include rock quarrying by early San Quentin prisoners. Also at Red Rock, around 1854, a man named Selim E. Woodworth is said to have led a Robinson Crusoe-like existence—or perhaps he just had a shooting box.

In 1867 the Marin Islands, the Sisters, the Brothers and Red Rock were declared U.S. Military reservations, apparently as a gesture in the name of harbor defense. The Marin Islands and Red Rock are now privately owned; the Sisters and Brothers are still under government ownership.

North on Highway 101

North of San Rafael proper, in the large suburban communities developed starting in the early 1950's, names recall Marin history:

Lucas Valley for John Lucas, nephew and heir of Timothy (Don Timoteo) Murphy, whose land all this once was;

Don Timoteo School in Terra Linda, near St. Isabella's Church and School which occupy the site where the Lucas ranch house was located;

Santa Margarita Valley, Park, and School; Las Gallinas Creek, Avenue, and Golf Course, from the name of Don Timoteo's land grant, *Rancho San Pedro, Santa Margarita y Las Gallinas*;

Manuel T. Freitas Parkway and Park for the pioneer banker and land baron who succeeded John Lucas as owner of Santa Margarita Ranch;

Miller Creek for Irish-born James Miller, who arrived with his family by wagon train in 1845 and later settled in what is now Marinwood.

Not old but descriptive is the name Terra Linda: terra, Latin for land or earth, and linda, Spanish for pretty.

GUIDE DOGS FOR THE BLIND: This training school, for both guide dogs and their blind masters, was founded in Los Gatos in 1942 and moved five years later to the present 11-acre campus at 350 Los Ranchitos Road off Highway 101. New kennels, student dormitories and administration building were completed in 1971.

The guide dogs—German shepherds, yellow and black Labrador retrievers and golden retrievers—are bred and born on the premises. As puppies they are placed with 4-H Club families and then returned to the school for training before they are paired with blind persons. Students and dogs graduate together after training as teams.

The dogs are provided without cost to sightless persons by Guide Dogs for the Blind, Inc. Students come from various states of the U.S. plus Western Canada.

The school is open to visitors from 2 to 4 P.M. Monday through Friday. Group tours may be arranged. Graduation ceremonies, held every four weeks, also are open to the public (information: 479-4000).

MUSEUMS IN MARINWOOD: Two unusual museums are located adjacent to Miller Creek School at 2255 Las Gallinas Avenue. Both are listed on the National Register of Historic Places.

At the entrance on Las Gallinas stands Old Dixie Schoolhouse. Built in 1864 by pioneer James Miller as a one-room country school and with a second room added about 1869, the little white building stood for years on Highway 101 north of Miller Creek Road. Classes there ended in 1958. In 1971 the school was moved to the present site to begin a new career.

The Dixie Schoolhouse Foundation, organized to restore the building and establish a historical museum, appointed Mrs. Josephine Leary as administrator. It was Mrs. Leary who began the campaign to preserve the old school following her retirement after years of teaching in Dixie District schools, including the original Dixie Schoolhouse.

Visits to the old schoolhouse may be arranged (information: Alice Allair, 479-8881).

Miwok Archeological Preserve was founded in 1970 by local residents who became fascinated with the idea that the suburban area where they had lived for less than two decades was inhabited by Coast Miwok Indians more than 3,000 years ago. They decided to learn something about these native Californians, who left evidence of their culture in several shell mounds along Miller Creek.

The result was an organization called Miwok Archeological Preserve of Marin, formed to protect the largest of the mounds adjacent to Miller Creek School and to establish a permanent museum and education center.

The mound was discovered to contain numerous burials and hundreds of artifacts. It is believed to have been the central village and ceremonial site of the valley, with known occupation dating from about 1,000 B.C.

Tours of the mound may be arranged (information: 479-5501). Artifacts are on display in Miller Hall, multi-purpose building at Miller Creek School.

ST. VINCENT'S SCHOOL FOR BOYS (State Historical Landmark No. 630): On land deeded by Timothy Murphy, the Daughters of Charity of St. Vincent de Paul founded a small school in 1855 and named it for their patron. Priests succeeded them and over the years built the present school on St. Vincent's Drive off Highway 101.

Today's landmark buildings date from the late 1920's. The main landmark is an imposing chapel or church, Queen of the Holy Rosary, dedicated in 1930, with stained glass windows, altar and statues of white marble, and three-inch-thick oak doors. The chapel and other structures are built around formal Italian-style gardens.

[80]

St. Vincent's was an orphanage for many years and is now a school and home for some 150 temporarily dependent boys of 6 to 16. St. Vincent's is also a working ranch; beef cattle are raised for school use and oat hay is grown for market.

The school grounds, where a historical marker was placed in 1958, are open to visitors. Group tours may be arranged (information: 479-8831). ∂∽

North Marin

Ignacio

The community of Ignacio was named for Ignacio Pacheco, who in 1840 received the 6,600-acre land grant *Rancho San Jose* (Spanish for Saint Joseph).

In early Marin history Pacheco is known not only as a former Mexican Army sergeant who became a prominent Marin *ranchero* and justice of the peace at the pueblo of San Rafael, but as the man who challenged Captain John C. Fremont to a duel and got away with it.

It was in 1846, according to the story, that Fremont arrived at the Pacheco rancho to requisition livestock for his troops. Pacheco had been warned ahead of time and had sent his best cattle and horses to a friend's rancho. What the furious Fremont had to say made Pacheco mad in turn, and he challenged Fremont to a duel with pistols or swords. But there was no duel; Fremont got back on his horse and galloped away.

The Pacheco adobe *hacienda* was located about 100 feet southeast of the present Galli's Restaurant. Some of the original foundations of the house, destroyed by fire in 1916, are still to be seen. The tree-lined drive to the restaurant is part of the drive which once led to the *hacienda*.

Frank Galli, proprietor of the restaurant, is former president of the Marin Historical Society and is sometimes called the mayor of Ignacio because of his dedication to the cause of preserving the area's identity through historic names. He approves of the name Alvarado for a neighboring inn since it honors Juan Bautista Alvarado, governor of Mexican California 1836–1842.

Ignacio Pacheco's son, Gumesindo, built a large Victorian home in 1881 at the present 5495 Redwood Highway which is now occupied by his descendants. The house is opposite Hamilton Air Force Base, where Gumesindo's race horses were trained.

HAMILTON AIR FORCE BASE: A bomber base known as Hamilton Field was dedicated by Brig. Gen. Henry H. 'Hap' Arnold of the U.S. Army Air Corps in 1935.

By that time the base had been operational for two years and Marin residents were accustomed to the name Hamilton, for Lieut. Lloyd A. Hamilton, Air Corps pilot killed in combat in France during World War I. He was a New Yorker, and there was considerable grumbling at first that a soldier from Marin or at least the Bay Area was not honored.

Hamilton Field was a bomber base until 1940 and then became a base for fighter units. During World War II hundreds of planes and thousands of men used the field.

When the Army Air Corps became the U.S. Air Force in 1947, the name was changed to Hamilton Air Force Base.

Today Hamilton, occupying 2,090 acres, is an Aerospace Defense Command base. Convair F-106 Delta Darts, supersonic jets of the 84th Fighter Interceptor Squadron, provide defense for Northern California.

Hamilton is also headquarters for numerous other activities including those of the Western Air Force Reserve Region, the Pacific Region and Marin Squadron of the Civil Air

Patrol, and the Aerospace Rescue and Recovery Squadron.

NOTE: Phasing out of the base to reserve status was announced in April, 1973.

HUMANE EDUCATION CENTER: Located on a seven-acre site at 171 Bel Marin Keys Road, this animal-and-education center opened in 1968 and is operated by the Marin County Humane Society.

The educational program is designed to teach humane attitudes toward animals of all kinds. Groups of children visit the center for tours and discussions, to meet the animal residents, and to learn about wild animals in the local environment. Classes include training in the care of domestic animals.

The center is headquarters for the Humane Society's traditional jobs of rescuing and caring for lost, injured or unwanted animals, returning lost pets, and placing animals in new homes. A fleet of animal ambulances operates 24 hours a day.

The Marin Humane Society, incorporated in 1907, serves as poundkeeper for the county and 11 cities.

The center with its kennels, corral-barn and indoor displays is open to visitors from 8.30 A.M. to 5 P.M. Monday through Saturday.

INDIAN VALLEY COLLEGES: A 333-acre site near the intersection of San Jose Boulevard and Sunset Parkway will be occupied by the Indian Valley Colleges, North Marin sister campus of the College of Marin.

Indian Valley will be a cluster of separate schools of study, initially three and eventually as many as eight.

Interim classes started with the 1971–72 term. Target date for opening in new buildings on the campus is 1975. ∞

Black Point

The name of Marin's northernmost community is said to date from the time of the early explorers, who called the point black because of its dark appearance from the presence of heavy oak forests. The giant oaks were timbered off for ships built at the Mare Island Navy yards in the 1860's.

Ships also were built here in the past, and Black Point was a major shipping point for lumber and livestock as well as a station on the railroad branching from Ignacio. Today only freight trains use the Northwestern Pacific tracks and Petaluma River bridge.

There was a Black Point post office twice, 1865–1891–when it served the entire Black Point-Novato area since Novato had no post office during those years–and 1944–1952. In between, 1905–1944, the post office was known as Grandview, apparently because a subdivider disliked the historic name of Black Point. Grandview survived as the name of an avenue.

Black Point Inn is a well-known historical landmark; a sign says 'since 1880.' The inn originally was a home for construction workers on the Petaluma River railroad drawbridge and in its early years served also as the local store, post office, train station and church.

BLACK POINT BOAT LAUNCH: Located in the shadow of the high bridge crossing the Petaluma River via State Route 37, this public launching ramp for boats opened in 1962 and is operated by the county. The half-acre-plus site is leased from the State Division of Highways. ❧

Novato

Incorporated 1960; area 22.56 square miles; 1973 population 32,900; post office established 1856, closed 1860, re-opened 1891.

When Novato was incorporated, city officials found a ready-made civic center at Sherman, DeLong and Machin Avenues. A former Presbyterian Church dating from 1896 is the city hall; two adjacent residences are used by city departments; the Novato Community House built in 1923 is now city property.

The old church was painted dark red with white trim, as were the other buildings, and today is the most photogenic of Marin's city halls. The interior was remodeled for offices and decorated in Victorian motif. On the walls are paintings and dozens of historical photos.

The civic center is located in the area that grew around the railroad station after passenger trains started running in 1879 and was part of the town of Novato laid out ten years later. Since this area dates back so many years it is Old Town to some residents, and merchants on Grant Avenue east of Highway 101 have formed an Oldtown Association.

But to local historians, the area east of 101 is New Town—new, that is, compared with the original Old Town on what is now South Novato Boulevard, where the earliest businesses were located. Boats and barges once could come this far on Novato Creek.

The original north-south road through Novato was via South Novato Boulevard, and this remained the main route until Highway 101 was opened on the present alignment in 1930.

Novato's first post office, 1856–1860, was in the original Old Town. The home of the first postmaster, Henry F. Jones, on what is now South Novato Boulevard near Yukon Way, also may have served as the post office—and Henry Jones may have been the 'Harry Jones' found murdered in a horse trough in 1872. In any event, the postmaster's home has been preserved; in 1972 it was donated to the city by Fabian Bobo and moved to a site near the city hall.

Today the latest (1968) Novato Post Office is in the Nave Shopping Center on South Novato Boulevard, not far from the location of the first post office.

Novato has an abundance of historic street names. Fernando and Feliz Lanes, for example, were named for the earliest settler and rancher, Fernando Feliz. In 1839 he was granted *Rancho de Novato(a)*, said to have been named for Saint Novatus.

Avenues were named for Joseph B. Sweetser and Francis C. DeLong, who in the mid-1850's bought some 15,000 acres of land and established huge orchards and dairy ranches. Around 1870 they built an 18-room mansion later owned by Robert H. Trumbull, a prominent resident for whom an avenue was named. The mansion still stands on a knoll at 50 Rica Vista and is presently owned by John Novak.

Sweetser donated land in the early 1860's for Pioneer Memorial Cemetery. No longer used for burials, it is now part of Pioneer Memorial City Park.

Numerous names including a shopping center, court, drive and bowling lanes honor Peter Nave, who arrived from Italy in the 1880's and operated a famous truck garden called the Cabbage Patch on the site of the present Nave Gardens residential area.

Machin Avenue bears the name of Timothy N. Machin, lieutenant-governor of California in 1863 who later went into the real estate business in Novato and then San Francisco.

But no street was named for Judge Herman Rudolff. In the 1920's the judge held court in the back room of his Novato French Cheese Factory, a landmark on Railroad Avenue now gone. Novato in those days was known as a 'speed trap' because the local constable stopped unwary motorists who failed to observe the 15-mile-an-hour speed limit. They were fined $10. The judge also performed marriage ceremonies at his factory.

Novato's newest (1971) public building is the regional branch of the Marin County Free Library at 1720 Novato Boulevard. Architects were Marquis and Stoller.

A popular event in Novato since 1955 has been the Western Weekend Country Fair, staged in June with western-style trappings such as a 'buckaroo breakfast' and melodrama, plus crowning of a queen, parade and carnival.

NOVATO PREHISTORY MUSEUM: Coast Miwok Indian artifacts, geologic specimens, scientific and historical collections are on display at this museum in Miwok City Park, Novato Boulevard and San Miguel Way.

The museum is operated by the Marin Museum Society, Inc., outgrowth of an archeological club at Novato High School. Crocker Bank donated the building which was moved to the site and remodeled under sponsorship of the Novato Kiwanis Club.

The museum is open to visitors from 10 A.M. to 2 P.M. Saturdays (information: 897-4064).

GNOSS FIELD (Marin County Airport): In 1939 a single small plane began using a new landing strip two miles north of Novato on Highway 101. Today this is Gnoss Field, now occupying nearly 100 acres, with modern runways, buildings and facilities.

Gnoss Field was dedicated in 1969 and named in honor of William A. Gnoss, county supervisor 1958–1971 and champion of the cause of a county airport.

Others prominent in the field's history are William Q. Wright, who prepared the first landing strip; P. W. (Woody) Binford, who opened a small airport and flying school in 1945; and Harry Tollefson, manager 1950–1968.

Just south of the airport is Black John Slough, named for a man known as Black John who had a house there in the 1850's.

RANCHO OLOMPALI (State Historical Landmark No. 210): Legend is mingled with fact in the nearly 700-year story of this area 3.5 miles north of Novato on Highway 101.

Coast Miwok Indians were here first, starting around 1300 A.D. Legend says that their large village called Olompali (o-LOM-pa-li) was visited in 1776 by Spanish soldiers, who were made so welcome that they taught the Indians how to make adobe bricks with which to build a home for their chief. Historians have argued this point, and recent research places the building of the first adobe as about 1824. Some of its walls still stand.

Camillo Ynitia, son of the chief, was the only native Indian in Marin to receive a Mexican land grant: *Rancho Olompali*, nearly 9,000 acres of his ancestral land.

The one shooting skirmish of the Bear Flag Revolt took place at Olompali in 1846 when American Bear Flaggers invaded the rancho to rescue some of their men who had been taken prisoner, and were met by Mexican California soldiers. The latter retreated after this 'Battle of Olompali' with one man killed and several wounded. An old tree still shows a cross slashed in the bark as a reminder of the casualty.

Camillo died in 1856–murdered, legend says, by another Indian or by a scorned woman. Another legend concerns gold buried on Mount Burdell, but none has ever been found.

Before his death, Camillo sold most of his holdings to land baron James Black, who gave the greater part of the rancho to his daughter Mary on her marriage to Dr. Galen Burdell, a San Francisco dentist. The Burdells operated big orchards, vineyards and 17 dairies, and in the 1870's planted Marin's first formal garden. Their home incorporated Camillo's three-room adobe.

After Dr. and Mrs. Burdell died, their son James inherited the ranch. In 1913 he tore down his parents' wooden home and replaced it with a 26-room stucco mansion, encasing the adobe within its walls. The mansion and home ranch were sold by his widow in 1943.

In recent years the mansion served in turn as a retreat for priests, a private club, and haven for a hippie colony. Fire made a shell of the mansion in 1969 but the adobe walls survived.

In 1972 a campaign was launched to preserve part of the area as a public historical park, and Rancho Olompali was placed on the National Register of Historic Places.

MIRA MONTE MARINA: Located on Highway 101 opposite Rancho Olompali, the privately-owned marina's docks and boat houses are built on the banks of tule-bordered San Antonio Creek near the point where it flows into the Petaluma River. The name originated with the Mira Monte Club organized in 1895 by James Burdell of Rancho Olompali and a group of his hunter friends. Their clubhouse on round, tree-covered Burdell Island burned down.

Legend has it that this area was the burial place of Indian chiefs and that bootleggers hid here during the 1920's.

STAFFORD LAKE COUNTY PARK: Eight miles west of Novato on Stafford Lake is Marin's largest county park in land area: 127 acres. Acquisition of land by the county began in 1968 and the park was dedicated in 1972.

The lake is owned by the North Marin County Water District and was dedicated in 1952 in honor of Dr. Charles Stafford, longtime Novato veterinarian, district board member and leader in the move to build the lake. He died in 1955.

HISTORIC VALLEYS: Two large valleys west of Novato have a particular flavor of the past: Hicks and Chileno. This was ranching country in the early days of Marin as it is today.

Hicks Valley was named for William Hicks, an early rancher. In 1865 Jefferson A. Thompson, an Ohioan who had come west by wagon train, bought 700 acres and started a business that is still operating: the Marin French Cheese Company on the Point Reyes-Petaluma Road near the junction of Novato Boulevard.

Today this is the sole survivor of half a dozen cheese factories once operated in Marin; the only milk-processing plant left in the county; and one of only two Marin members of the 100-Year Club sponsored by the California State Exposition and state Chamber of Commerce. (The other member is the daily *Independent-Journal*, tracing its ancestry to the *Marin County Journal* founded in 1861.)

[91]

The cheese company is now operated by the founder's grandsons. With its factory tours and picnic grounds, it is a major attraction for Marin residents and visitors.

Chileno Valley was named for a colony of 'Chilenos,' the popular term for Chilean-born residents who arrived in the 1860's. Earlier there was a settlement called Spanish Town around the intersection of the present Marshall-Petaluma and Chileno Valley Roads.

Marin's three surviving one-room schools, Laguna, Lincoln, and Union, are located in these valleys. They are separate school districts which extend into Sonoma County.

North of Chileno Valley is the Two Rock Military Reservation, on 800-plus acres mostly in Sonoma County. The base formerly was part of an Army communications network and was taken over in 1971 by the U. S. Coast Guard as a training center. ๛

Stinson Beach

Post Office established 1916

The long expanse of white sand and crashing breakers at Stinson Beach, with the slopes of Mount Tamalpais in the background, have attracted visitors since the days of horse and buggy and stagecoach.

Several place names were associated with this area before the name Stinson Beach became official. First it was part of *Rancho las Baulenes*, then a rancho called the Belvidere– today, spelled Belvedere, the name of an avenue–and then Stinson's Rancho.

For years the beach itself was known as Easkoot's, for Captain Alfred D. Easkoot, master mariner, first county surveyor, and eccentric recluse. In the 1880's Easkoot guarded the beach with a shotgun and fired a warning shot at any beachcomber who picked up driftwood. The home built by the captain in 1875 still stands on Highway 1 (Shoreline Highway) at the corner of Calle del Pinos.

Around the turn of the century and later, the beach was called Willow Camp, and hundreds pitched tents there. The original Willow Camp was in the beach area opposite the Superette–formerly Airey's, first grocery in town–on Highway 1, and is now part of Stinson Beach State Park.

The permanent name for the beach and village honors Nathan H. Stinson, whose 1906 subdivision called Stinson Beach was the start of today's community. Nathan's brother Amos and his wife gave land for a school, now a youth center. Their daughters donated the site for the Stinson Beach Community Center, Community Church and Volunteer Fire Department on Belvedere Avenue off Highway 1.

Dedicated in 1953, the Community Center is the scene of varied activities including the Stinson Beach Wildflower Show, an annual spring event from 1958 to 1973.

The annual Dipsea Race which begins in Mill Valley ends at Stinson Beach. The first race was held in 1905 when, it is said, a group of hardy men decided to run nearly seven miles over the mountain for a dip in the sea.

STINSON BEACH STATE PARK: In 1932, Justice of the Peace Archie H. Upton, Nathan Stinson's stepson, agent, and one of his heirs, donated to Marin County the first acreage of what was to be the state beach. Willow Camp was purchased by the county in 1939 at the urging of the Marin Conservation League, and ten years later the county turned over both areas to the state. Stinson Beach State Park opened in 1950 and now includes some 53 acres.

Now for day use only with no camping as there was in the old days, Stinson is a favorite with picnickers, hikers, swimmers, surfers, fishermen, and beach explorers.

Adjoining the beach is a long sandspit separating Bolinas Bay from Bolinas Lagoon. In 1911, a branch of the Mount Tamalpais and Muir Woods Railway was planned, but abandoned, to run down the mountain and over the sandspit with a drawbridge across the channel to Bolinas. Later an offer was made to sell the sandspit to the state but was refused. Today the sandspit is Seadrift, an area of private beach homes with a locked gate.

AUDUBON CANYON RANCH: Located on Highway 1 three miles north of Stinson Beach, the 1,000-acre ranch with its four canyons is the result of a campaign launched by the Marin Audubon Society in 1961 to preserve a major nesting area for great blue herons and American egrets. The ranch is now operated as a joint project by the Marin, Golden Gate and Sequoia Audubon Societies.

Headquarters are in a two-story white ranch house with a gabled roof, built in 1875 by Captain Peter L. Bourne. A milking barn added in the early 1930's has been converted into a hall for exhibits relating to the birds and nesting area, Bolinas Lagoon where the birds feed, local history, geology and botany, plus a nature book shop. Parking and picnic areas are located in the ranch yard.

The birds' nests in the tops of tall redwood trees are visible from ranch headquarters. A short, steep trail leads to an overlook where mounted telescopes provide close-up views from above—a thrill even for visitors who are not 'bird watchers.'

Volunteer Canyon, used as a wildlife education center, includes an 1875 ranch house built by Samuel P. Weeks and his carpenter shop dating from 1852.

In 1968 Audubon Canyon Ranch was designated a Registered Natural Landmark by the National Park Service.

The ranch is open to visitors from 10 A.M. to 4 P.M. on weekends and holidays during the nesting season, March 1-July 4. Tours by school children and other groups may be arranged for Tuesday through Friday, October 1-July 4 (information: 383-1644).

BOLINAS LAGOON COUNTY PARK: This 1,034-acre park in and around the scenic lagoon includes Kent Island (110 acres) and tidelands donated by conservation groups, more tidelands acquired with state and federal funds, and 824 acres turned over to the county after the Bolinas Harbor District was dissolved in 1969.

A plan adopted by the county in 1972 designates the lagoon as an ecological preserve and calls for trails, observation points, nature centers, and areas for parking and picnicking.

BOLINAS LIGHTER WHARF SITE (State Historical Landmark No. 221): In the early 1850's, when numerous sawmills operated in this area, lumber was hauled by oxteam out of the canyons and off the ridges to wharves at the north end of Bolinas Lagoon. There the lumber was loaded on flat-bottomed boats called lighters to be carried to seagoing vessels waiting offshore.

Today only a few pilings sticking up out of the water near the head of the lagoon mark the location of the old wharves. The site is on the Olema-Bolinas Road a short distance from its junction with Highway 1. There is no historical marker.

Point Reyes Peninsula

This huge (100-square mile), triangle-shaped peninsula jutting out into the Pacific is probably the most photographed, most written-about place in all of Marin.

Geologically the peninsula is a definite unit separated from the mainland by the San Andreas fault zone, which extends from Bolinas Lagoon through the Olema Valley and Tomales Bay. The peninsula has moved slowly northward along this fault for some 80 million years. Rocks on the peninsula are different from those on the mainland; there is remarkable variety in the climate, landscape, wildlife, trees and plants—and spectacular scenery.

There is also an intriguing historical mystery: was it here that the English explorer and privateer Francis Drake landed nearly four centuries ago in his treasure-laden *Golden Hind*? Many historians, but not all, believe that Drake sailed his little vessel into what is now called Drakes Bay on June 17, 1579, careened her on the beach for repairs, visited with the friendly Indians, and claimed the land for England and Queen Elizabeth. Drake's crew built a fort that historians are still looking for.

Two other early ships of note put into Drakes Bay: in 1595 the galleon *San Agustin*, commanded by Sebastian Rodriguez Cermeño, which was blown ashore and thereby accounted for the first recorded shipwreck on the California coast; and in 1603 the *Capitana*, whose commander, Sebastian Vizcaino, left a permanent name. Since the day of arrival was January 6, the day of the Three Holy Kings, he called the point *Punta de los Reyes* or Point of the Kings.

Another name dates from 1841, when the Mexican trader *Ayacucho* went aground on what is now called Limantour Spit for her French commander, Jose Yves Limantour.

Coast Miwok Indians in large numbers first lived on the peninsula; 113 of their village sites have been discovered. In the early 1830's white settlers began to arrive, and in 1858 two brothers and law partners, Oscar L. and James McMillan Shafter, became sole owners of the vast peninsula. They divided their holdings into about two dozen dairy ranches, and for 60 years most of the land was kept intact by the family. Sales to individual ranchers began in 1919.

On Point Reyes Peninsula today are the communities of Bolinas and Inverness, a national seashore, parks, and other places of interest. ∞

Bolinas

Post Office established 1863

Bolinas is one of Marin's oldest towns, with a rollicking past.

In 1850 Bolinas was the biggest and busiest place in the county. Of the 323 inhabitants counted that year in the first U. S. census of Marin, two-thirds were in Bolinas Township. They were mostly men busy cutting down the big trees, milling the logs and shipping the lumber to San Francisco—much of it on schooners built right here.

Before the arrival of the loggers and their noisy saws, Bolinas was the quiet Mexican *Rancho las Baulenes* (a name probably of Indian origin.) Two former soldiers, Rafael Garcia in 1836 and Gregorio Briones ten years later, raised cattle for hides and tallow and enjoyed the leisurely life of the day. More cattle were brought in after lumbering ended, dairy cattle this time, and dairy ranching flourished—but today there are no more dairy ranches at Bolinas.

Stagecoaches began clattering in regularly during the 1870's to connect Bolinas and its sheltered beach with the towns on the other side of the mountain. Starting in the early 1880's, summer homes could be built in a subdivision laid out near the beach by Mr. and Mrs. Frank Waterhouse. Today the original houses are still there together with newer homes.

Expansion to the mesas or plateaus above the town proper began in 1909 with a subdivision on what is called the little mesa, above Brighton Avenue and Wharf Road. The biggest subdivision was in 1927 on the big mesa: more than 5,400 lots on 300 acres. The 20 x 100-foot lots sold for $69.50 apiece to persons who subscribed to the San Francisco *Bulletin*.

Bolinas buildings from the past include:

St. Mary Magdalen Catholic Church, Olema-Bolinas Road near the junction of Upper Road, built in 1878. The Presbyterians and Methodists built nearby the same year and residents called the area Gospel Flat.

Calvary Presbyterian Church, moved to the present site on Brighton Avenue in 1898. The Methodist Church was dismantled in 1909 and moved to Wharf Road, where it is now the Sharon Building.

Bolinas School, on the Olema-Bolinas Road approaching the village, built in 1907 and identical to the 1867 school which stood on the same spot. A modern school in the rear is now used for classes.

Christian Science Church near the school, dating from the 1870's when it was a Druids Hall.

Smiley's Bar on Main Street, formerly the Schooner Saloon with the original part of the building dating from 1852. Bolinas once had nine saloons.

Gibson House Restaurant, Main Street, built in 1875 by postmaster-store owner John Charles Gibson as a new home. His store went down in the 1906 earthquake and the present general store is on the same site.

Californiana Galleries, Wharf Road, originally the Adams Hotel built about 1880.

College of Marin Marine Station, Wharf Road, the former U. S. Coast Guard station (1917–1946). A few pilings remain from the wharf at the other end of the road where Captain Louis Petar tied up the passenger-and-freight schooner *Owl* between trips to San Francisco, from 1911 until the early 1930's.

BOLINAS PARK: The county's smallest park (.68 acre) is on Brighton Avenue near the beach, with a tennis court that has been used by generations of Bolinas residents and summer visitors. The park was included in an 1883 subdivision laid out by Mr. and Mrs. Frank Waterhouse and was donated to the county by their daughter, Marin Waterhouse Pepper (Mrs. Lewis G. Pepper), in 1933.

RCA AND COAST GUARD RADIO STATIONS: RCA, formerly located at Marshall (page 111), moved its transmitters in 1930 to Mesa Road, two-plus miles from the Olema-Bolinas Road junction, and the receiving station to the west side of Point Reyes Peninsula (page 106). These are now operated by RCA Global Communications, a subsidiary of the Radio Corporation of America. High-frequency equipment is used to communicate with places thousands of miles away in the Pacific and with ships at sea.

The U. S. Coast Guard in 1971–1972 built its principal radio facility for the Pacific in the same areas: transmitters just north of RCA at Bolinas, receiving station next door to RCA on Point Reyes Peninsula. The new facility was designed to handle messages, monitor ships in distress, and expedite search-and-rescue operations.

The Coast Guard stations are open weekends, 1 to 4p.m.

POINT REYES BIRD OBSERVATORY: The only bird observatory in North America in operation the year around has its headquarters at the end of Mesa Road four miles from the intersection of the Olema-Bolinas Road, in the southern extremity of Point Reyes National Seashore.

Point Reyes Bird Observatory was founded here in 1965 for the study of land birds, shore birds and waterfowl, and their environment. Three years later a second research station was established on Southeast Farallon Island, 30 miles off the Golden Gate.

The headquarters site is in the old Palomarin Ranch, once the settlement of a religious group known as Christ's Church of the Golden Rule. The settlement's school is now the observatory headquarters building.

The Bolinas site, including a reception center and display room in the headquarters building, is open to visitors every day of the week except Monday. Visits by school children and other groups are by appointment (868-1221).

AGATE BEACH COUNTY PARK: The main feature of this unusual county beach–on nearly seven acres with 1,200 feet of ocean front–is the chance to study marine life at low tide on the rocks and in the tidal pools of Duxbury Reef.

Visitors are asked to help preserve the natural life of the reef by not taking away any marine specimens–tidepool collecting is, in fact, against the law. Fishing off the beach and rocks is permitted.

The reef and point were named for the *Duxbury*, which went aground on the reef in 1849. Seven more groundings and shipwrecks followed, the last in 1914.

The Agate Beach property was donated to the county in 1964 by the Bolinas Public Utilities District. Access is from a parking area at the end of Elm Road. ✌

Inverness

Post Office established 1897

The community of Inverness was founded in 1889 when James McMillan Shafter subdivided 640 acres of his Point Reyes land as a summer colony. He gave it a Scottish name because his family originally came from Scotland and added street names like Argyle, Aberdeen, Cameron, and Dundee.

In 1897 the first village store opened in Inverness. The second floor collapsed on the first floor in the 1906 earthquake but was propped up and repaired, and a good-as-new building resulted. It still stands 'downtown' on Sir Francis Drake Boulevard, occupied by the post office plus a gift shop and art gallery.

St. Columba's Episcopal Church, dating from 1903, was named for the sixth century apostle to the Scottish Highlanders. The congregation moved in 1951 from a small chapel to the remodeled Robert B. Frick mansion on Sir Francis Drake Boulevard, originally built in 1930.

St. Columba's Church and its amphitheater are the scene of the popular Inverness Music Festival held every summer since 1965. Another well-known local event is the annual Primrose Tea given in the early spring by the Inverness Garden Club.

The Inverness Association holds title to a local landmark, the 1910-vintage Brock Schreiber boathouse on Tomales Bay. The boathouse is about a quarter-mile south of the Inverness Yacht Club, which dates from 1912.

Today Inverness is still a resort community with old and modern summer and week-end homes, several well-known restaurants, and places for visitors to stay.

About half of the residents of both Inverness and Inverness Park, where development started in 1909, live there the year around. Many of the older homes on the wooded hillsides of Inverness still display, in the old manner, names like Edgemont, The Laurels, The Gables, and Quail Point.

TOMALES BAY STATE PARK: The start of this park near Inverness was Shell Beach, purchased by Marin County in 1945 half with county funds and half with private donations raised by the Marin Conservation League with the cooperation of other groups. More acreage was added in 1951 with county and state funds, again plus private subscriptions. Tomales Bay State Park opened in 1952 with 1,018 acres.

The day-use-only park includes two miles of shoreline on Tomales Bay, trails, abundant plant and wildlife, and a grove of ancient, craggy Bishop pines that is one of the finest left from California's prehistoric forests.

Beaches in addition to Shell are named Pebble, Heart's Desire, and Indian. Parking and picnic areas and dressing rooms are in and near Heart's Desire Beach. Access to Shell Beach, separated from the other beach areas by private property, is via Camino del Mar off Sir Francis Drake Boulevard.

POINT REYES NATIONAL SEASHORE: First proposed by the National Park Service in 1935, the seashore became a reality in the 1960's at the urging of conservationists in Marin and Washington and after a battle to save the peninsula from land speculators. President John F. Kennedy signed the seashore bill on September 13, 1962. He was scheduled to visit Point Reyes in November of 1963 but plans were changed; instead, he went to Dallas.

On September 20, 1966, the seashore was dedicated by Mrs. Lyndon B. Johnson in a ceremony at Drakes Beach.

More than 54,500 acres of land plus 10,400 acres of tidelands are within the seashore boundaries. Included are nearly 14,000 acres leased to ranchers, about 380 acres used by the U. S. Coast Guard and Federal Aviation Agency, and some 3,800 acres in private ownership.

Seashore headquarters are located about a mile west of Olema in Bear Valley. The big red barn near the Information Center is on the site of the original barn which was torn in half by the 1906 earthquake along the San Andreas Fault. To study the fault, visitors may see a working seismograph in the Information Center and walk along the self-guiding Earthquake Trail with signs pointing out changes in the landscape as a result of the big 1906 quake.

Bear Valley was the private domain of a hunting club from 1890 to the early 1930's. Today it is the gateway to more than 100 miles of trails through the scenic valley, to the high country, to the ocean, and to four pack-in camps (reservations: seashore headquarters). Bicyclists as well as hikers use the Bear Valley and Coast Trails and horseback riders are permitted on all of the trails except the Bear Valley Trail on week-ends and holidays. Both bicycles and horses are for rent near the seashore. On summer week-ends and holidays, the park service operates free shuttle bus service between Bear Valley and Limantour Spit.

Near the trailhead in Bear Valley is the Morgan Horse

Farm, dedicated in 1970, where horses are bred and trained as mounts for the rangers (and one rangerette) who patrol the trails, beaches and campgrounds, and for use in other national parks.

Laguna Ranch, once used for dairying and during World War II by the U. S. Infantry, is now the site of two camps: an American Youth Hostel and NEED (National Environmental Education Development), for students of Marin, Sonoma and Alameda County schools.

Of the beaches the most protected from wind is Drakes Beach, with picnic and parking areas and a modern Visitor Center. Here also are the white cliffs along the shore that may have been seen by Francis Drake and his *Golden Hind* crew in 1579. A monument was erected in 1946 to commemorate the landing.

An area of 52 acres in the rear of Drakes Beach formerly was a county park. The land was purchased in 1938 with funds contributed by Marin residents and deeded to the county.

Also a former county park is McClure's Beach, donated in 1942 by Mrs. Margaret McClure. This and the 52 acres at Drakes Beach are now part of the seashore. McClure's is reached after a half-mile hike down a canyon from the parking area at the end of Pierce Point Road.

On the west side of the peninsula are Point Reyes Beach North and South, beautiful with pounding surf and favored by hikers, beachcombers and fishermen, but too dangerous for swimming, surfing, or even wading.

SCHOONER BAY: During the heydey of Point Reyes ranches, schooners came in on the tide to Drakes Estero and then Schooner Bay to load boxes of butter and other ranch products for the San Francisco market.

Oystering in the estero dates from the early 1930's, and today, across from the old schooner landing, the Johnson

Oyster Company raises giant Pacific oysters on 1,000 acres of leased tidelands. Most of the production is by the Japanese-developed hanging culture method in which seed oysters are strung on wire over wooden frames and sunk into deep water. In the past almost the entire planting was from Japanese seed, but in recent years most of the seed oysters have come from Dabob Bay, Washington.

RADIO RECEIVING STATIONS: Clusters of high poles mark the locations of three radio receiving stations half way down the peninsula off Sir Francis Drake Boulevard.

RCA Global Communications and the U. S. Coast Guard have receiving stations here and transmitters at Bolinas (page 101).

Third station is the AT&T Receiving Station for radio-telephone communication. High frequency radio transmissions are received from ships at sea and far-away places like Tokyo, Hong Kong and Tahiti. The calls are then channeled into the U. S. direct-distance-dialing system.

American Telephone and Telegraph Company, Long Lines division, has operated a receiving station at this site since 1931.

The AT&T station is open to visitors, depending on the work load. Inquiries may be made via the telephone at the gate.

POINT REYES LIGHTHOUSE: The lighthouse on the western tip of Point Reyes Peninsula has been in service since 1870 to help ships navigate safely past the high, rocky headlands. Most of them have, but since according to official records this is the foggiest spot and one of the windiest on the California coast, there have been numerous shipwrecks. Thirty-eight wrecks were recorded, 1595–1935, on Point Reyes, Point Reyes Beach and in Drakes Bay. ๛

RETURNING TO HIGHWAY 1: about a mile north of the Olema-Bolinas Road junction is the site of a settlement which grew up in the 1850's during the heydey of lumbering. An ox-team road led to the sawmills on Bolinas Ridge and a copper mine midway to the ridge, through what is still called Copper Mine Gulch.

Lumbermen named the settlement Woodville. Market hunters, who hunted wild game to sell, later congregated here. They owned so many dogs that the area was nicknamed Dogtown. The Dogtown Pottery now marks the entrance to Copper Mine Gulch.

OLEMA LIME KILNS (State Historical Landmark No. 222). A legend that these kilns were built early in the 1800's either by the Russians or the Spanish led to their being made a state landmark. Later research revealed that the kilns were built by two Marin County men in 1850, that they probably were not fired more than a dozen times, and that it is doubtful if any of their lime ever reached the market.

The site is on private property about four miles south of Olema, is not marked, and is not open to the public. ◌

Olema

Post Office established 1859

Olema, named for the Coast Miwok Indian village of Olema-loke (Coyote Valley), was one of Marin's most important early towns. By the mid-1860's the town boasted not only its own post office, one of half a dozen in the county, but a large grocery, butcher shop, livery stables, and even a dry goods store. There were two hotels known for their hospitable landlords.

With the opening of the North Pacific Coast Railroad in 1875, Olema's importance began to fade. The route bypassed the town and went instead through what was called Olema Station, now Point Reyes Station.

Ironically, Olema's most famous citizen, James McMillan Shafter, was first president of the railroad. Shafter was a prominent attorney and later San Francisco Superior Court judge as well as one of the owners of the huge Point Reyes ranches. His showplace mansion in Olema called The Oaks, built in 1869, has been preserved.

Both Olema hotels burned down in 1876, and the next year a new hotel was built by stageline-owner John Nelson at the corner of what are now called Sir Francis Drake Boulevard and Highway 1. Condemned as a fire hazard, the old building was saved by a new owner in 1972 and scheduled to be restored.

One historic Olema building, or part of it, is missing: the false front of a butcher shop which stood for a century or so on Highway 1 opposite the present Sacred Heart rectory. Since 1967 the missing bit of old Olema has been in the Smithsonian Institution, national museum of history and technology in Washington, D. C. The shop facade is now the background and centerpiece for an exhibit called 'The Character of the Old West' in the Hall of Everyday Life in the American Past.

Today Olema's business section consists of one restaurant-bar and an old false-front building occupied by the post office and an antique shop, with a grocery next door. The 1881 Druids Hall nearby has been restored as a private home. Down the road near the entrance to Point Reyes National Seashore is the new (1969) Olema Ranch Campground, where campers, trailers and tents are seen on what was once an artichoke field. ஒ

Point Reyes Station

Post Office established 1882

This was a stop on the railroad from the day North Pacific Coast trains started running in 1875. Since there was no town on the site at the time, and stagecoaches to Olema connected with the trains, the stop was called Olema Station. In 1883 the name was changed to Point Reyes Station.

Also in 1883 the townsite was laid out by Dr. Galen Burdell, known as the founder of the community.

Burdell, a dentist who lived at Rancho Olompali near Novato, inserted a clause in the deeds to his town lots that made history in the field of anti-trust laws. Purchasers were forbidden to sell liquor. But Burdell did, at his Point Reyes Hotel and saloon built in the early 1880's. He had a monopoly until Salvatore Grandi opened another saloon in his store across the street in 1902. Burdell sued–and lost.

The Point Reyes Hotel was located on the site of the present Grandi Company building on A Street at Second. Across Second Street was the Grandi store and saloon, now restored as The Western.

The present brick Grandi structure, dating from 1906,

[109]

originally included a hotel, with the lobby and dining room downstairs and guest rooms above. In 1940 a U.S. Army colonel by the name of Dwight D. Eisenhower stopped there while on maneuvers at Point Reyes. Colonel Eisenhower played bridge in front of a fireplace still in the Grandi store.

In 1933 the trains stopped running and today the main thoroughfare, A Street, follows the railroad right-of-way which went through the middle of town. The Silver Dollar, West Marin Medical Clinic and *Point Reyes Light* office stand where tracks used to be. Nearby in its original location is the old depot.

At the end of A Street the old railroad engine house has been converted into a Community Center. Activities there include the annual West Marin Junior Livestock Show in June, sponsored by the West Marin Lions Club and first held in 1949.

Near the Community Center is the Foresters Hall, built about 1914, now the Sandcastle Gallery. Another landmark is the 1914 Sacred Heart Catholic Church, used for parish activities since a new church was built at Olema in 1967.

TWO HISTORIC SPOTS: In the early 1860's Samuel P. Taylor built a warehouse and landing on Lagunitas Creek at what is now the junction of Highway 1 and Sir Francis Drake Boulevard near Point Reyes Station; the West Marin Real Estate office is located there. Flat-bottomed boats came up the creek from Tomales Bay to deliver rags for Taylor's Pioneer Paper Mill (Samuel P. Taylor Park) and to pick up paper. Later he shipped by wagon and train.

The second site, historic especially to geologists, is on Sir Francis Drake Boulevard about a quarter-mile southwest of the Highway 1 junction. It was here that the greatest lateral movement of the 1906 earthquake occurred along the San Andreas fault. The ground moved 20 feet. ๙

[110]

Along Tomales Bay's Eastern Shore

From 1875 until early in 1930, trains ran on narrow-gauge tracks along the eastern shore of Tomales Bay. The scenic route for train passengers along most of the length of the 15-mile-long bay is the same for motorists now on Highway 1. Names on the map remain from the days of the railroad, and stretches of right-of-way for the tracks may still be seen.

Highway 1 winds past open water, fishing docks, boat works, a marina, cottages on the shore, the site of an early radio station, a town more than a century old, and a county park. Oyster companies, open to the public, are located near Bivalve and Ocean Roar.

There are two seafood restaurants, at Reynolds, a stop on the railroad possibly named for cattleman William Reynolds, and Nick's Cove, near Hamlet, named for land-owner John Hamlet. Another stop was at Millerton, probably named for landowner James Miller.

Marconi was the site of a radio station operated by the Marconi Wireless Telegraph Company and then RCA (pages 101 and 106), 1914–1930. The company built a large two-story hotel which is now part of the Synanon Foundation's 'communal city'. Synanon bought the property in 1964 and has added modern buildings.

Marshall

Post Office established 1872

Marshall, an important shipping point during the days of the railroad, was named for Samuel, Hugh, James and Alexander Marshall, four brothers from Ireland who began ranching in the early 1860's. The first store opened in 1867 and by 1880 the town had two stores, a blacksmith shop, hotel and post office.

In Marshall today are one store, in the same old false-front building with the post office and a beer-and-wine bar; an art gallery in what used to be a coal-and-feed dealer's; and a jewler's shop in a former boat works. Nearby is the Marshall Tavern, spared when the landmark Marshall Hotel next door burned down in 1971 after standing nearly a century.

St. Helen's Catholic Church, on a hill above Marshall on the Marshall-Petaluma Road, dates from 1902.

Several areas along Tomales Bay were acquired by conservationists in 1972 to hold as wildlife and ecological preserves. They include Audubon Cypress Grove, purchased by Audubon Canyon Ranch, a 75-acre complex of land, marsh and tidelands. A 30-acre section of the complex was acquired with the help of the Marin Conservation League as a memorial to Mrs. Norman Livermore, a founder of the league and its second president.

Farther north in Tomales Bay, Audubon Ranch purchased two-acre Hog Island, plus smaller Duck Island and six acres of tidelands, to preserve as public open space.

MILLER PARK: The six-acre county park at Nick's Cove includes a picnic area set among cypress trees on a bluff looking over Tomales Bay, and a public boat launching ramp and fishing access on the shore. Mrs. Fred Miller donated the site to the county in 1955.

Highway 1 from Miller Park follows an estuary and creek known to historians as Keys, for John Keys, who in 1850 sailed up the then-navigable stream in his small schooner *Spray* and built the first structure in the Tomales settlement (page 114.) Numerous maps, including official county maps and those of the North Pacific Coast Railroad, used the name Keys. On most modern maps the name is given only to the creek above its fork with Walker Creek (at Walker Creek bridge), named for rancher Lewis W. Walker.

To local residents and to county engineers, the creek from this fork down to the bay is now 'Walker Creek,' since the main flow of water comes from that stream. Walker Creek is the county's second largest (after Lagunitas Creek) in volume of flow and watershed area.

Two miles north of Miller Park is a reminder of the days of the railroad: iron piers from a bridge across Keys (or Walker) Creek. Camp Pistolesi, about half a mile farther on, once was a popular summer resort. A narrow bridge across the creek marks the location.

The entire 118-acre delta of the creek and the estuary, from old Camp Pistolesi to the mouth of the estuary at Tomales Bay, plus two acres of land along the creek shore, were acquired in 1972 by Audubon Canyon Ranch as a wildlife sanctuary. ✼

Tomales

Post Office established 1854

Of the early Marin towns, Tomales was second in importance only to the county seat of San Rafael–and a busy shipping point as well. Huge quantities of ranch products were shipped annually, first on schooners which sailed up Keys (Walker) Estuary and Creek (page 114) from Tomales Bay, and starting in 1875 on the North Pacific Coast Railroad.

The estuary and creek were first called Keys for a young Irishman, John Keys, who arrived in 1850. His 'shake shanty' was the start of the original Tomales settlement, at what is now the junction of Highway 1 and the Tomales-Petaluma Road.

Keys, with an 1852 arrival, Warren Dutton, opened the first store in 1854 in Keys's shanty. The settlement grew; an 1859 map of the Keys Embarcadero in the Marin County Historical Society Museum shows ten warehouses, a large hotel, post office-store-hall, and other buildings. A fleet of schooners operated to and from San Francisco.

This original settlement was called Lower Town after Keys and Dutton parted company and Dutton opened a store in 1858 in Upper Town, the present Tomales business section on Highway 1. The two 'towns' were rivals for years, but silting in the creek ended the days of the embarcadero by the early 1870's, and then trains took over. Today the only business place in 'Lower Town' is a service station-store. The silted-in creek bed is used for grazing, although water still makes channels through the pasture. The old Keys home still overlooks the once-busy area from a knoll above the intersection of Highway 1 and the Tomales-Petaluma Road.

By 1880, in what became the permanent town of Tomales, there were two hotels, stores, a cheese factory, bank and numerous saloons. Today Tomales still has an old-fashioned flavor, with older homes, a general store, Diekmann's, in a building which dates from the 1870's; the post office, oldest in Marin except for San Rafael, next door; a branch of the Bank of America; a coffee shop, the Village Inn, in a former butcher shop; and one bar, the William Tell House, on the site of the original saloon of the same name which was re-built after the 1906 earthquake and again after a fire in 1920.

Center of community activities is Tomales Town Hall,

located on land deeded by Warren Dutton in the 1870's.
The hall is the next-to-last building on the east side of
Highway 1 going north.

Two of Marin's most historic churches are in Tomales.
Church of the Assumption (Catholic), on Highway 1 just
south of the business section, was built in 1860 on land
given by John Keys. The building was shaken from its
foundations in 1906 but was restored, and today is still an
active parish church.

Tomales Presbyterian Church, on Church Street above
Highway 1, was built in 1868 to replace an 1866 structure
destroyed by fire. The land was donated by Warren Dutton.
One of the original trustees was George W. Burbank, whose
younger brother Luther, the famed horticulturalist, lived
and experimented on a nearby ranch before moving to Santa
Rosa in 1878. Members of the Burbank family still live in
the Tomales area.

The name Tomales is said to be of Indian origin, derived
from the word tamal for bay. The Tomalenos (Tamalenos,
Tamallos) Indians lived along the coast. Another theory is
that the name originated because Spanish explorers found
that the Indians made a tamale-like food from wild seeds.

FALLON: Located about two miles north of Tomales, this was an early settlement named for a pioneer family. Fallon was a stop on the railroad; James L. Fallon shipped potatoes on the first train to carry ranch products out of the area. At the present Fallon Store on Whitaker Bluff Road off Highway 1–with a post office dating from 1898–locomotives took on water. The water tank may still be seen.

ELEPHANT ROCKS: South of Tomales on the road to Dillon Beach is a group of well-known natural landmarks called Elephant Rocks. They were etched out, according to geologists, by slow erosion of the surrounding land from rain and wind. ௸

Dillon Beach

Post Office established 1923

This long-time resort community on Bodega Bay was named for a pioneer rancher from Ireland, George Dillon, who settled here in 1859.

The bay itself was named for–and by–a Spanish explorer, Lieut. Juan Francisco de la Bodega y Cuadra. As commander of the schooner *Sonora*, one of several Spanish vessels exploring the northern coast, he directed his little ship into the bay on October 3, 1775, and to overnight anchorage at the mouth of Tomales Bay. The Sonoma County fishing port of Bodega Harbor and two Sonoma towns, Bodega Bay and Bodega, later were named for him.

Russians arrived on the scene in 1811 and called Bodega Bay 'Port Romanzov'–fortunately a temporary name. They built warehouses, sent out Aleut Indians in their sealskin canoes to trap sea otters for the Russian-American Fur Company, and used the bay as a shipping point for the

Russian colony at Fort Ross. In 1841, having killed off most of the sea otters, the Russian abandoned both Fort Ross and Port Romanzov.

A place name going back to the mid-1840's is Tom's Point, for Thomas Wood, first white settler in Tomales Township. Known as Tom Vaquero because of his skill with horse and riata, Wood settled with Coast Miwok Indians at a rancheria on the point later named for him, and married an Indian girl. Today Lawson's Landing resort is located between Tom's Point and Sand Point.

Shipwrecks are part of the local story: 11 were recorded in Tomales and Bodega Bays, 1852–1906.

Bodega Bay and Harbor were dedicated in 1970 as State Historical Landmark No. 833, and a plaque was placed in Doran (Sonoma County) Park on the north side of the bay.

PACIFIC MARINE STATION: An abundance of marine life in the Dillon Beach vicinity has made it a mecca for marine scientists and students for more than 60 years. The permanent station on Cliff Street in Dillon Beach was established in 1947.

A division of the University of the Pacific at Stockton, the station offers a year-around program of instruction and research for undergraduates and a graduate program leading to the Master of Science degree.

Three buildings with laboratories, classrooms, offices and living quarters are on the site. The station's four boats include a 42-foot research vessel. ∞

APPENDIX I
Marin's Railroads

Railroads are frequently mentioned in *Discovering Marin*, since they are part of the story of the county and of almost every town. The railroads were a key factor in Marin's growth from only 6,900 inhabitants in 1870 when the first train appeared to nearly 53,000 in 1940 as the era of passenger trains and connecting ferryboats was about to end.

Only a few decades ago, Marin residents could commute to San Francisco by electric train and ferryboat, and take vacation trips north on trains pulled by steam locomotives with melodious whistles. Automobiles, buses and the Golden Gate Bridge spelled the doom of the interurban trains and big ferryboats. Service north was cut as more and more travelers chose the highway over the railway until, in 1958, the one surviving passenger train out of Marin made its last run.

Northwestern Pacific or 'NWP' was Marin's sole rail line from 1907 until the end of the passenger trains, as it is with the freight service remaining today. The railroads which preceded NWP included the colorful North Pacific Coast with its narrow-gauge tracks–three feet between rails, explains historian A. Bray Dickinson,[1] compared with the standard-gauge four feet, eight and one-half inches. North Pacific Coast trains and ferries competed with those of the second major railroad on the scene, San Francisco & North Pacific; eventually, both lines were absorbed by NWP.

Following is a brief chronology of Marin passenger train service as it appeared and then disappeared.

[1]In *Narrow Gauge to the Redwoods.* Other rail and ferry histories are *Redwood Railways* by Gilbert H. Kneiss; *The Northwestern Pacific Railroad* by Fred A. Stindt and Guy L. Dunscomb; and *San Francisco Bay Ferryboats* by George H. Harlan.

[118]

1870–San Rafael & San Quentin Railroad started train operations between San Rafael and ferryboat landing at San Quentin Point.

1875–North Pacific Coast Railroad established rail-ferry terminal at Sausalito. Trains began running over a wooden trestle across Richardson Bay to Strawberry Point (abandoned 1884 for new route), Corte Madera, Tamalpais (Ross), San Anselmo (then known as Junction, where a branch line took off for San Rafael), Fairfax, San Geronimo Valley, Olema Station (Point Reyes Station), along the shore of Tomales Bay, to Tomales.

North Pacific Coast Railroad took over the San Rafael & San Quentin. (Ferry landing at San Quentin used until 1884.)

1879–San Francisco & North Pacific Railroad extended line south from Sonoma County to Novato, Ignacio and San Rafael.

1884–San Francisco & North Pacific extended line from San Rafael to Tiburon, where a rail-ferry terminal was established.

1888–Trains began running over line from Ignacio to Black Point and Sonoma County; later part of San Francisco & North Pacific.

1889–North Pacific Coast Railroad completed branch line to Mill Valley.

1902–North Pacific Coast reorganized as North Shore Railroad.

1903–North Shore began electrifying interurban lines.

1907–Northwestern Pacific Railroad formed by merger of North Shore, San Francisco & North Pacific, and other companies. NWP, owned by Southern Pacific and Santa Fe Railroads, linked the Bay Area with the Redwood Empire.

1909–NWP passenger terminal shifted from Tiburon to Sausalito; Tiburon became freight and mechanical terminal.

1929–Southern Pacific became sole owner of NWP.

1930–Service from Point Reyes Station to Tomales and Sonoma County points discontinued.

1933–Service on line between Fairfax and Point Reyes Station discontinued.

1937–Golden Gate Bridge opened.

1940–Service on Mill Valley branch line discontinued.

1941–Trains on remainder of electric lines and ferryboats between Sausalito and San Francisco discontinued. San Rafael became NWP southern passenger terminal.

1958–Last passenger train from San Rafael to Willits, on NWP main line, discontinued.

APPENDIX II
Major Parks, Museums & Landmarks

Parks
NATIONAL
Golden Gate National Recreation Area
Muir Woods National Monument
Point Reyes National Seashore

STATE
Angel Island*
Marin Headlands*
Mount Tamalpais*
Muir Beach*
Samuel P. Taylor
Stinson Beach*
Tomales Bay

COUNTY
Agate Beach
Black Point Boat Launch
Bolinas Lagoon

*In Golden Gate National Recreation Area

COUNTY PARKS (continued)
Bolinas Park
Civic Center
Deer Park
Harbor Cove Nature Preserve
John F. McInnis Park
McNear's Beach
Miller Park
Muir Beach Overlook
Nicasio Point Nature Preserve
Old St. Hilary's Historic Preserve
Paradise Beach
Stafford Lake Park
Tiburon Uplands Nature Preserve

Museums
Audubon Canyon Ranch
Louise A. Boyd Marin Museum of Science
Marin County Historical Society Museum
Marin Museum Association Gallery
Mission San Rafael Replica
Miwok Archeological Preserve
Novato Prehistory Museum
Old Dixie Schoolhouse
Old St. Hilary's Historic Preserve
San Geronimo Railway Station

Historic Places & Landmarks
NATIONAL REGISTER OF HISTORIC PLACES
Angel Island
(Old) Dixie Schoolhouse
Forts Baker, Barry and Cronkhite
Miwok Archeological Preserve
Rancho Olompali
Robert Dollar Estate

[121]

NATIONAL REGISTER OF NATURAL LANDMARKS
Audubon Canyon Ranch

STATE HISTORICAL LANDMARKS
Angel Island
John Reed's Sawmill
Mission San Rafael Replica
Olema Lime Kilns
Rancho Olompali
Site of Bolinas Lighter Wharves
Site of Lord Fairfax Home
Site of Pioneer Paper Mill
St. Vincent's School for Boys

STATE POINT OF HISTORIC INTEREST
Old St. Hilary's Historic Preserve

Bibliography

BATY, DAVID R. 'Point Reyes Station's Great Monopoly Case.' *Independent-Journal* Marin Magazine, May 14, 1966.

BROWN, STUART E., Jr. *Virginia Baron.* Story of Thomas, 6th Lord Fairfax. Chesapeake Book Co., Berryville, Va., 1965.

California Historical Landmarks. State Department of Parks and Recreation, Sacramento, 1971.

Deeds and Maps. Marin County Recorder's Office, Civic Center.

DICKINSON, A. BRAY. *Narrow Gauge to the Redwoods.* History of the North Pacific Coast Railroad. Trans-Anglo Books, Los Angeles, 1967.

DONNELLY, FLORENCE. History of San Rafael. *Independent-Journal* Marin Magazine, Jan. 10, 24 and 31, 1970.

DONNELLY, FLORENCE. 'Tomales: Marin's 100 Year Old Settlement.' *Independent-Journal* Marin Magazine, Oct. 28, 1950.

DWYER, JOHN T. *One Hundred Years An Orphan.* St. Vincent's School for Boys, 1855–1955. Academy Library Guild, Fresno, 1955.

EVANS, ELLIOT. Chronology of Angel Island. *Report and Recommendations on Angel Island.* Marshall McDonald Associates, Oakland, 1966.

FINNIE, RICHARD. *Marinship.* Marinship Corporation, 1947.

FORBES, JACK D. *Native Americans of California and Nevada.* Naturegraph Publishers, Healdsburg, 1969.

GARDINER, DOROTHY. 'It All Started with Four Women.' Story of the Marin Conservation League. *Independent-Journal* Marin Magazine, March 7, 1964.

GEARY, IDA. *Marin Trails.* The Tamal Land Press, Fairfax, 1969.

GILLIAM, HAROLD. *Island in Time: the Point Reyes Peninsula.* Sierra Club, 1962.

GUDDE, EDWIN G. *California Place Names*. University of California Press, 1965.

HARLAN, GEORGE H. *San Francisco Bay Ferryboats*. Howell-North Books, Berkeley, 1967.

Here Today: San Francisco's Architectural Heritage. Junior League of San Francisco, Inc. Chronicle Books, San Francisco, 1968.

Historic Spots in California. Third edition. Revised by William N. Abeloe. Stanford University Press, 1970.

HOWELL, JOHN THOMAS, and PHYLLIS ELLMAN. *Saint Hilary's Garden*. Belvedere-Tiburon Landmarks Society, 1972.

IACOPI, ROBERT. *Earthquake Country*. Lane Books, Menlo Park, 1969.

KNEISS, GILBERT H. *Redwood Railways*. Howell-North, Berkeley, 1956.

LAMOTT, KENNETH. *Chronicles of San Quentin*. David McKay Company, New York, 1961.

'Land Grants and Brands of Marin County.' Map and chart. Marin County Historical Society, 1972.

Land Use Survey, Proposed Point Reyes National Seashore. National Park Service, U.S. Department of the Interior, 1961.

LITTLE, LUCRETIA H. *The Mill That Shouldn't Have Been*. City of Mill Valley, 1967.

LITTLE, LUCRETIA H. 'There's A Mystery to the Mission.' *Independent-Journal* Marin Magazine, Dec. 9, 1967.

MASON, JACK, with HELEN VAN CLEAVE PARK. *Early Marin*. House of Printing, Petaluma, 1971.

MASON, JACK, with THOMAS J. BARFIELD. *Last Stage for Bolinas*. North Shore Books, Point Reyes Station, 1973.

MASON, JACK. *Point Reyes, the Solemn Land*. DeWolfe Printing, Point Reyes Station, 1970.

MUNRO-FRASER, J. P. *History of Marin County*. Alley Bowen & Company, New York, 1880.

Novato Advance. Tenth City Anniversary Edition Feb. 4, 1970.

PEPPER, MARIN WATERHOUSE. *Bolinas. A Narrative of the Days of the Dons*. Vantage Press, New York, 1965.

Post Office Records. National Archives and Post Office Department Library, Washington, D.C.

REVERE, JOSEPH W. *Keel and Saddle*. James R. Osgood & Company, Boston, 1872.

Sausalito. Guidebook. John Edeen, 1972.

SECCHITANO, JEAN. 'Golden Days of Fairfax, 1831–1931.' Fairfax Central P-TA, 1962.

Shark Point-High Point. History of Tiburon and Belvedere by 8th Graders of Reed Union School District, 1954–1958. Revised edition. Reed District Parent-Teacher Club, 1970.

SLAYMAKER, CHARLES M. *Cry for Olompali*. 1972.

STINDT, FRED A., and GUY L. DUNSCOMB. *The Northwestern Pacific Railroad*. 1964.

TEATHER, LOUISE. *Island of Six Names*. History of Belvedere, 1834–1890. Belvedere-Tiburon Landmarks Society, 1969.

THARP, LOUISE HALL. *Three Saints and A Sinner*. Story of Julia Ward Howe, her sisters Louise and Annie (Mailliard) and their brother Sam. Little, Brown & Company, Boston, 1956.

TREGANZA, ADAN E. 'Old Lime Kilns Near Olema.' *Geologic Guidebook of the San Francisco Bay Counties*. State Division of Mines, 1951.

U.S. Coast Pilot 7: Pacific Coast. Coast & Geodetic Survey, U.S. Department of Commerce, 1968.

Watershed Lands in the Mount Tamalpais District. Marin Municipal Water District, 1967.

WURM, T. G., and A. C. GRAVES. *The Crookedest Railroad in the World*. History of the Mt. Tamalpais & Muir Woods Railway. Howell-North Books, Berkeley, 1960.

Your County: Marin. League of Women Voters of Marin. 1971.

[125]

Index

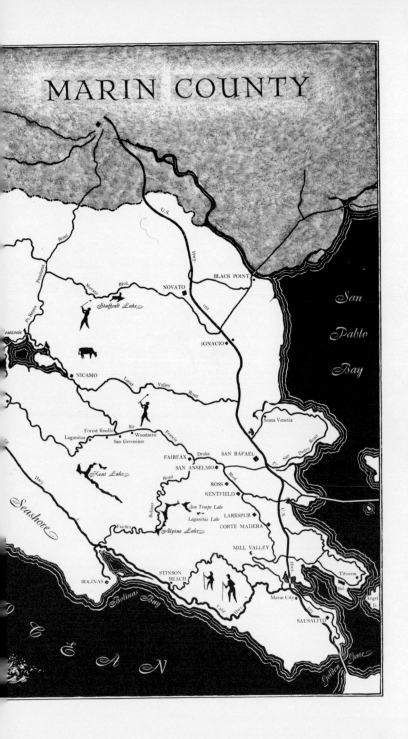